KING KONG

Conceived by
Edgar Wallace and **Merian C. Cooper**
Novelization by
Delos W. Lovelace

Grosset & Dunlap

GROSSET & DUNLAP
Published by the Penguin Group
Penguin Group (USA) Inc., 375 Hudson Street,
New York, New York 10014, U.S.A.
Penguin Group (Canada), 10 Alcorn Avenue, Toronto, Ontario, Canada
M4V 3B2 (a division of Pearson Penguin Canada Inc.)
Penguin Books Ltd, 80 Strand, London WC2R 0RL, England
Penguin Ireland, 25 St Stephen's Green, Dublin 2, Ireland
(a division of Penguin Books Ltd)
Penguin Group (Australia), 250 Camberwell Road, Camberwell, Victoria
3124, Australia (a division of Pearson Australia Group Pty Ltd)
Penguin Books India Pvt Ltd, 11 Community Centre,
Panchsheel Park, New Delhi - 110 017, India
Penguin Group (NZ), Cnr Airborne and Rosedale Roads, Albany,
Auckland 1310, New Zealand (a division of Pearson New Zealand Ltd)
Penguin Books (South Africa) (Pty) Ltd, 24 Sturdee Avenue, Rosebank,
Johannesburg 2196, South Africa

Penguin Books Ltd, Registered Offices:
80 Strand, London WC2R 0RL, England

Published in 2005 by Grosset & Dunlap, a division of Penguin Young
Readers Group, 345 Hudson Street, New York, New York 10014.
GROSSET & DUNLAP is a trademark of Penguin Group (USA) Inc.

Printed in the United States of America

ISBN 0-448-43913-1

1 3 5 7 9 10 8 6 4 2

Chapter 1

Even in the obscuring twilight, and behind the lightly floating veil of snow, the Wanderer was clearly no more than a humble old tramp freighter. The most imaginative, the most romantic eye could have detected nowhere about her that lean grace, those sharply cleaving contours which the landsman looks for in a craft all set to embark upon a desperate adventure.

For the likes of her, the down-at-heels support of the Hoboken pier was plenty good enough. There, with others of her kind, she blended into the nondescript background of the unpretentious old town: she was camouflaged into a comfortable nonentity. There she was secure from any embarrassing comparison with the great lady-liners which lifted regal and immaculate prows into the shadows of skyscrapers on the distant, Manhattan side of the river.

Her crew knew that deep in her heart beat engines fit and able to push her blunt old nose ahead at a sweet fourteen knots, come Hell or high water. They knew too that surrounding her engines, and surrounding also that deep steel chamber which puzzled all of them and frightened not a few, was a staunch and solid hull. Landsmen, however, drawn to the waterfront by that nostalgia which every so often stirs those whose lives are bound by little desks and brief commuter train rides, looked over her rusted, scaling flanks and sputtered ignorantly:

"Lord! They don't call that a sea-going craft, I hope!"

Weston, though he had taxied to the waterfront bent upon a business in which nostalgia had no part, said exactly that and drew back the hand which had been about to pass over the fare from Forty-second Street and Broadway. After all, if he had mistaken the pier, it would be a foolish extravagance to let this pirate on wheels knock down his flag and so gain the right to add an extra fifteen cents to the return charge.

Hanging tightly to his money, he lumbered out of the taxi with that short-winded dignity which marks the fat man of fifty-odd. In the same moment, an old watchman poked a cold red nose around the corner of a warehouse.

Weston hailed him:

"Hi, Cap! Is that the moving picture ship?"

Only after the cold red nose had bobbed assent did Weston pass over the cab fare, and even then there was a glint of suspicious doubt in his eye. Still hardly more than half satisfied that he had not mistaken the rendezvous, he scuffed through the light fall of snow to the Wanderer's gangway.

" 're you another one agoin' on this crazy voyage?" the old watchman demanded suddenly from the gloomy shadow of the warehouse.

"Crazy?" Weston swung around the more quickly because the adjective bolstered a conviction that had been growing in his own mind. "What's crazy about it?"

"Well, for one thing, the feller that's bossin' it."

"Denham?"

"That's him! A feller that if he wants a picture of a lion'll walk right up and tell it to look pleasant. If that ain't crazy, I want to know?"

Weston chuckled. That wasn't so far from his own estimate of the doughty director of the Wanderer's destinies.

"He's a tough egg, all right," he agreed. "But why the talk about this voyage being crazy?"

"Because it is, that's why."

The watchman emerged from his snug, protected niche the better to pursue the conversation.

"Everybody around the dock—and lemme tell you there're some smart men around here even if they ain't got such high and mighty jobs—everybody around the dock says it's crazy. Take the cargo this Denham's stowed away! There's stuff down there I can't believe yet, and I seen it go aboard with my own two eyes. And take the crew! It's three times too big for the ship. Why it'll take shoe horns to fit 'em all in!"

He paused but only for breath. Plainly he was prepared to bark out an interminable succession of charges against the Wanderer. Before he could reopen his critical barrage, however, a young authoritative voice put a permanent stop to it.

"Hey, on the gangway there! What do you want?"

Weston looked up toward the low deck rail amidship. Light streaming from a cabin astern and higher up outlined a figure; and in the illumination Weston felt sure, from Denham's descriptions, that he was seeing the Wanderer's personable first mate. There, unmistakably, was the long, young body Denham had praised. There were the reckless eyes, the full strong mouth. Weston, whose experiences had taught him to guard against spontaneous regard for any stranger, however personable, yielded for once to a swift liking. There, he admitted, was as pleasant a young fellow as a man could hope to meet—as any woman could hope to meet, he added, on second glance.

"What do you want?" the brisk demand came down a second time as Weston made his inspection.

"Want to come aboard, Mister Driscoll," Weston replied; and grown a little more cheerful because of his liking for the mate he began a cautious ascent of the wet and slippery gangway.

"Oh, you must be Weston."

"Broadway's one and only," Weston admitted. "Weston, the ace of theatrical agents, even if," he added as he began to puff a little from the ascent, "my wind is not what it used to be."

"Come aboard! Come aboard!" cried Driscoll. "Denham's wild to hear from you. Have you found the girl?"

In the darkness Weston's cheer evaporated. He made a wry face and said nothing, but followed Driscoll's springing stride aft and up a ladder to the lighted cabin.

This low enclosure was invitingly spick and span, but it was furnished with the spartan simplicity which characterizes womanless quarters. The sole decorations were a mirror on one wall and a well filled pipe rack on another, unless one counted an overcoat or two with attendant hats. For the rest there were only four chairs, an oblong table of the broad squat sort favored by men who like to spread out maps for studying, an open box containing black corrugated iron spheres larger than oranges but smaller than grapefruit, and a brightly polished brass cuspidor which stood close by a foot of one of the two men waiting in the cabin.

This man was lean, and of no more than middle height. Behind a heavy moustache, his hard jaw worked slowly upon a generous mouthful of plug cut. He was in vest and shirtsleeves. Above these a captain's uniform cap lent an air of command, but this did not keep him from stepping definitely aside in order to leave the center of the stage to his companion.

His companion was just such a well tailored, well-groomed man of thirty-five as you might run into at any stockbroker's desk; although there you would rarely encounter such an air of solid power, of indomitable will. Bright brown eyes, shining with an unquenchable zest for the adventure of living, flashed toward Weston as he entered, and an impatient voice said without preliminary:

"Weston! I was just going ashore to ring you up."

"If I'd known that I'd have waited," Weston answered, eyeing his wet shoes.

"Shake hands with the Skipper, Captain Englehorn," Denham pushed on.

The man in the captain's cap, turning from a center shot into the bright cuspidor, held out a rough, thick hand and after it had been shaken moved the box of corrugated iron spheres to make more room at the table for Weston's chair.

"I take it you're already acquainted with Jack," Denham added, and as Weston nodded smilingly at Driscoll who smiled back, he went on, "Well! Then you've met a pair you'd never come across on Broadway, Old Man. Both of them were with me on my last two trips and I'll tell you if they weren't going on this one I'd think a long time before I started."

There fell that little restless silence which always burdens men upon whom extreme praise has been bestowed. Then Denham dropped into his chair and eyed the theatrical agent.

"Where's the girl, Weston?"

"Haven't got one."

"What!" Denham struck the table. "Look here, Weston! The Actors' Equity and the Hays outfit have warned every girl I've tried to hire. And every agent but you has backed away. You're all I've got left. You know I'm square. . . ."

"Everybody knows you're square," Weston grunted, breathing audibly. "But everybody knows, also, how reckless you are. And on top of that can you hope to inspire confidence about this particular voyage when you're so secretive?"

"There's truth!" drawled Englehorn, and leaned down to his cuspidor.

"Absolutely!" cried Driscoll, rubbing his handsome young jaw. "Why not even the Skipper and the mate know where this old ship's going . . ."

"There you are!" Weston spread his palms up. "Think of my reputation, Denham. I can't send a young, pretty girl, or for that matter even a homely one if you'd have her, on a job like this without telling her what to expect."

"And what is she to expect?" Denham demanded.

"To go off for no one knows how long, to some spot you won't even hint at . . . the only woman on a ship that carries the toughest mugs my wise old Broadway eyes ever looked up and down."

As the other three grinned the agent added hastily, "Of course I mean the crew."

"Weston!" Denham's fist crashed onto the table again. "I'm going out to do the biggest thing in my life and I've got to have that girl."

"You never had a woman in any of your other pictures. Why do you want one for this?"

"Hell's Bells! You don't think I'm consulting my own preference, I hope."

"Then, why. . . ."

"Why? The Public's why! My blessed Public must have a pretty girl's face. Romance isn't romance, adventure is as dull as dishwater . . . to my Public . . . unless, every so often, a face to sink a thousand ships, or is it saps? shows up. Imagine! I slave, I sweat blood to make a fine picture. And then the Public says: 'We'd have liked it twice as much if there'd been a girl in it.' And the exhibitors say: 'If he'd given us a real love interest, the picture would have grossed twice as much.'

"All right!" Denham's fist hit the table one last, decisive thump. "They want a girl. I'll give them a girl."

The dark declaration of the old watchman returned to Weston. Denham wasn't, of course, crazy. But just the same his present plan was not one a theatrical agent who cared for his reputation ought to help along.

"Sorry!" he said, and picked up his hat. "I don't believe there's anything I can do for you."

"You've got to do a lot," Denham said, "and in a hurry. We have to sail on the morning tide. We must be out of here by daylight."

"Why?"

"I guess it won't do any harm to tell you now," Denham decided irritably. "We're carrying explosives. And the insurance company has found out. If we don't get away on the jump a marshal's deputy will be on our necks. And then there'll be a legal row and we'll be tied up for months."

His mood changed suddenly, and going over to the box that Englehorn had pushed aside he picked up one of the iron spheres. He looked at it with a proud, possessive grin.

"Far be it from me," he said, "to tell you,

Weston, that any girl you'd find for me would meet with no danger on this expedition. Of course there'll be a little now and then. Maybe," he conceded with a broader grin, "more than a little. But take this from me! So long as we have a couple of these handy, nothing very serious can happen."

"What have you got there?"

"Gas bombs, Old Man! My own prescription. Or perhaps I should say my own improvement upon standard models. Gas bombs powerful enough to knock a row of elephants for a loop."

"W-What?" Weston stammered. "Denham, everything I hear makes me like this business less. I'm beginning to be glad I didn't find you a girl."

"Don't be like the insurance company," Denham said scornfully. "Don't worry about a little explosive. There's no more harm in these than in so many lollypops as long as they are handled by men who understand their little ways—men like Jack there, or the Skipper, or myself. The truth is, Weston, plain rain and the monsoon season are likely to cause us a lot more trouble and danger."

"M-Monsoons!"

"Sure! They're another reason why I've got to get my girl and start instantly. I can, of course, trust the Skipper to take the Wanderer through a blow; and Jack, too!" Denham paused for an affectionate slap at Driscoll's broad back.

"But the monsoons bring rain, and rain ruins an outdoor picture. It wastes months, wastes money, and leaves a man with nothing to show for all his work."

"M-Monsoons! G-Gas bombs!" Weston was still stuttering. "By George! You make me feel like a potential murderer." He clapped his hat firmly onto his round head and reached for the doorknob. "Denham, you'll get no girl through me."

"What?"

"I mean it."

"You do, eh! Well, then I'll get one without you."

For so stocky and solid a man, Denham jerked an overcoat from one hook, a hat from another, with amazing speed.

"If you think I'm going to quit, just because you won't find me a girl with backbone. . . ."

He thrust Weston's plump bulk aside and jerked open the door.

" . . . I'm going to make the greatest picture in the world. Something that's never been seen; never even dreamed of. They'll have to invent new adjectives when I come back. You wait!"

The door jerked shut.

"Where are you going?" Englehorn cried.

Denham's indomitable voice floated back as the sound of his footsteps moved steadily down the ladder and to the gangway.

"I'm going out to find a girl for my picture.

I'm going to bring one back . . . if I have to kidnap her."

Inside the cabin Weston buttoned up his own overcoat, staring the while at Driscoll and Englehorn. He was more glad than ever that he had kept clear of the whole crazy mess. Crazy, he decided, was exactly the right word. The old watchman had been a lot more than half right.

Driscoll began to laugh.

"Bet you," he offered Englehorn, "that Denham gets his girl."

"I don't take the bet," said Englehorn, chewing calmly.

Driscoll turned to Weston, still laughing, white teeth flashing in his tanned face.

"He'd have the nerve to tell me to marry her if he decided the scenario called for it," he said. "Can I light you down to your cab?"

Chapter 2

Denham was searching for a face. Jostling through the Broadway theatre-hour crowds he waited, watched, and every once in a while swore impatiently under his breath because some especially promising countenance proved commonplace upon a second glance.

He concentrated upon faces, excluding all other details. With eyes closed to slits, like camera lenses, he caught, and poised for inspection, and discarded countless faces among the drifting hosts. Bold faces, frightened faces, sullen faces, inviting faces, pouting faces, expectant faces, painted faces, sordid faces, hard faces, indifferent faces. But nowhere did he discover a face which cried out: "Here I am. The one you are seeking."

Even Denham's resolute will was not proof
against such unfailing failure. In the end, with
a headshake which was close to despair and was
certainly the very peak of bitter disappointment,
he turned downtown. Tramping with gloomy
determination he left the bright incandescence
of Times Square and hunted through the canyon
of the lower avenue. Faces in murky doorways.
Faces on street corners. Faces on park benches.
Faces in bread lines. Faces in automobiles. Faces
in street cars. Neat faces. Soiled faces. Sad faces.
Gay faces. But never a face which would gleam,
like a candle flame, in the picture he was so
sure would be the greatest picture in the world.

Denham found he had circled back. Madison
Square's benches, and the faint but persisting
eternal light above them, were behind him. He
had combed Fifth Avenue, Park Avenue, swaggering, intimate Fifty-seventh Street. Now, in
the dreary upper west Forties, he was drifting
down again toward the Broadway crowds beginning to boil out of a hundred theatres and
motion-picture palaces.

Reluctant to face the certainty of renewed
failure among these, he decided to loiter over
a cigarette. He found his case empty, so he
stopped at a little sidewalk shop; and in the
ensuing weeks he was moved every once in a
while gravely to shake hands with himself over
the good luck which had caused him to do this.
It was a very little shop, hardly even a full

grown booth. It was scarcely large enough for
the swarthy unshaved proprietor and the more
perishable part of his stock in trade. It was so
small that a durable exhibit of apples had to be
displayed on a stand alongside.

Upon the apples the swarthy proprietor kept
a suspicious eye even while he sold Denham
the cigarettes. The apples were within Denham's
vision too. And, actually, it was he who first
saw what happened.

A girl came softly up to the apple stand and
reaching out a slim white hand began to close
it slowly and hungrily about the red fruit.

Denham saw it first: the swarthy proprietor,
however, was only the briefest glance behind,
and as his customer tore open a fresh pack of
cigarettes, he went through the booth's door
roaring.

"Ah-ha! So I catch you. You stealer! Ho! Ho!"
He seized the girl's wrist. "No, no, you don't
run. Hey! Where is-a da cop?"

"No!" The girl cried and pulled weakly away.
"Please let me go. I didn't take anything. I
wanted to but I didn't."

"Every hour somebody steal. Me! I've had
enough. Hey! Mister Cop!"

"Shut up!" Denham ordered. "The girl's telling the truth. She'd got her hand off your rotten
apple before ever you started out. She wasn't
going to steal anything."

"I wasn't. Truly, I wasn't."

"Here, Socrates," Denham commanded with finality. "Take this dollar and forget it."

The dollar completely reversed the swarthy proprietor's point of view. He seized it, dropped the girl's wrist and trotted back into his booth streaming thanks behind him.

So unexpectedly freed, the girl would have collapsed had not Denham flung an arm about her shoulders. Her head fell back. The booth's single electric bulb streamed light full upon it and for the first time a clear view of her face was possible. Denham looked. He looked again, and the eyes that had been so long half closed, opened wide. Still again he looked; then he laughed and squaring his shoulders triumphantly threw up a signalling hand.

"Taxi," he called. And when one pulled up to the curb with screeching brakes he ordered, "The nearest restaurant. And snap into it."

Half an hour later, in a white tiled lunch room around the corner, he still wore his air of triumph. In the chair opposite him, the girl sat behind a white barricade of empty plates and cups. She had not spoken while she ate, and Denham had not spoken either. Leaning forward on folded arms, he had stared in thankful contentment at her face.

It was more than a beautiful face, although it was beautiful, with the well-molded clearly defined features in which his cameraman's eye had immediately rejoiced. Large eyes of incredible blueness looked out at him from shadowing lashes; the ripe mouth had passion and humor; the lifted chin had courage. Her skin was transparently white; and not, Denham decided, because she was so plainly undernourished. That marvelous kind of skin belongs with the kind of hair which foamed up beneath her shabby hat. This was a pure gold. If Denham had been poetical, which he was not, he might have pictured it spun out of sunlight.

Facing his intent, gratified stare, she smiled.

"I'm a different Ann Darrow now," she said.

"Feeling better, eh?"

"Yes, thank you. You've been wonderfully kind."

"Don't give me too much credit," Denham said bluntly. "I'm not spending my time and money on you just out of kindness."

All the humor and most of the smile faded out of Ann's face. She shivered a little. Denham ignored her reaction.

"How come you're in this fix?"

"Bad luck, I guess. There are lots of girls just like me."

"Not such a lot who've got your looks."

"Oh, I can get by in good clothes, perhaps." Fear was still in Ann's smile. "But when a girl gets too shabby . . ."

"Any family?"

"I'm supposed to have an uncle . . . some-where."

"Ever do any acting?"

"A few extra jobs in the moving picture studio over at Fort Lee. Once I got a real part. The studio is closed down now."

He hazarded one more question.

"Are you the sort of city gal who screams at a mouse and faints at a snake?"

"I'm a country gal . . . Er, I wouldn't exactly choose to pet a mouse. But I killed a snake . . . once."

Denham squared his shoulders again in an even plainer triumph, and stood up.

"Listen, sister. I've got a job for you."

Ann stood up too, and meeting Denham's gaze returned it steadily and waited.

"When you're fed up, and rested, and all rigged out, you'll be just the type I want."

"When . . . when does the job start?"

"Now. This minute. And the first thing you do is get some new clothes. Come on. We ought to find the Broadway shops still open."

"But . . . but what is the job?"

"It's money, and adventure, and fame. It's the thrill of a lifetime. And a long sea voyage that starts at six o'clock come morning."

Ann sat down again and soberly shook her head. There was no fear in her face now. Instead there was a good-humored tolerance which she seemed able to call up easily from long practice.

"No! I'm sorry . . . But I can't . . . I do want a job so . . . I *was* starving . . . But I can't . . ."

"What?" cried Denham, and stared at her in amazement; then he laughed and reached for the cigarette he hadn't remembered to smoke since leaving the swarthy one's booth. "Oh, I see! Nope, sister. Nope. You've got me wrong. This is strictly business."

"Well," said Ann apologetically. "I didn't want any . . ."

"Any misunderstanding. Sure. Sure you didn't. It's all my fault, for getting excited and not explaining. So here's your explanation. I'm Denham. Ever hear of me?"

"Y-yes. Yes. You make moving pictures. In jungles and places."

"That's me. And I've picked you for the lead in my next picture. We sail at six."

"Where to?"

"I daren't tell you that for a while, Ann. It's a long way from here. And before we reach it, there'll be a long voyage, easy living, the warm blue sea, soft moonlight on the water. Think, Ann! No matter what comes at the finish, isn't that better than tramping New York? Afraid every night that the next morning will find you in the gutter?"

"No matter what comes at the finish," Ann whispered. "It's better."

"I'm square, Ann," Denham added. "And I'll be square with you. No funny business."

"You can't tell me yet what I'm to do?"

"Keep your chin up and trust me," Denham told her and held out his hand.

Ann looked at him for a long direct moment. Denham looked back at her. He was always lucky, he reminded himself, his grateful gaze sliding again over her bright hair, her perfect face, her graceful well-proportioned figure.

When his eyes came back to hers, Ann put her hand into his with a grave smile.

Chapter 3

Ann came wide awake in the narrow berth and for a little could not remember how she had got there. All she could think of was that this was the first morning in weeks that she had not awakened to hunger. Wondering what had happened to hunger, she recalled last night's amazing encounter and sat up. She laughed aloud when she spied beside her berth the bowl of apples.

Denham had bought them at the last moment, adding their bulk to a pile of dress boxes, shoe boxes and hat boxes that overflowed the taxi.

"And here's a bowl to put 'em in," he had said. This last when they came aboard, long after midnight, past the Wanderer's solitary watchman and a plainly suspicious old fellow with a cold red nose, who stood on the pier.

Bowl of apples in hand, she had tiptoed after Denham down a dim brief alley.

"This will be your cabin," he had said. "You'll find a key inside. Got it? Fine! Good night, sleep tight! And make it a long one. If I see you around before late afternoon I'll have the skipper put you into irons."

Ann brushed her foaming bright hair back from bright eyes and looked at the tiny clock which was an item in her cabin's equipment. It was a little short of eight. She had been in bed, then, some five or six hours. But except for this last little cat-nap she hadn't slept at all. She yawned and laughed again. A girl only half as excited as she was could scarcely have slept. And since there was no likelihood that she would be any less excited for hours she decided to go on deck, defying the irons of Mr. Denham's skipper.

He, she recalled from Denham's brief account of his assistants, would be Captain Englehorn. He was old and gruff, but nice. Driscoll, the mate, was young and gruff, Denham said, but a good sort, too.

She swung slim legs over the edge of the berth, stood up and went to the open porthole. Denham's promised departure had unquestionably been made at the scheduled six o'clock. New York had vanished. Land was visible low

down on the horizon to the stern. But off-ship
and forward there was only water. Calm water,
beneath a soft, placid sky. The snow of the
night before had vanished and along with it the
threat of stormy weather. The temperature was
up so much that standing there, in no more than
her thin nightgown, Ann was not very cold.

Turning away from the porthole, Ann fingered the nightgown with delight.

"Buy whatever you like, sister," Denham had
said. "You'll still come cheap, compared to what
I'd have had to pay anybody off Broadway or
out of Hollywood. Shoot the works."

So, bearing in mind that she would be away
from shops for months, Ann had taken him at
his word. Nightgowns. Underthings. Stockings.
Even lounging pajamas. And coats and dresses
and hats. And finally enough oddments to stock
a beauty specialist. And here they all were, in
a tottery mountain of boxes that the Wanderer's
earnestly throbbing engines threatened to bring
down about her knees at any moment.

She decided to open just one; and as a con-
sequence of that surrender to pleasure it was
nine o'clock and past before she closed the door
of her cabin and stepped out into a deserted
passageway.

Under a new coat she wore her own old dress
because she did not want Denham to think her
too eager to seize her newly found luxury. But
under the dress was a fresh, an immaculate

silken smoothness which caressed her from shoulders to toes.

"Really," she thought as she emerged onto the deck, "it's a downright pity they don't have automobiles on a ship. This is exactly the time for one to give me a little bump and turn me into an accident victim. I've never been in such a beautiful state of preparedness."

The deck was almost as deserted as the passageway had been. Even a lady landlubber did not need long to conclude that the officers and crew, having cleared away the business of departure, had gone about their various concerns below. Only one person was visible. Over in a sheltered corner, full in the warm rays of the climbing sun, sprawled a veritable Methuselah of a sailor, a brown, stringy, bald, old codger who hummed as he tied knots for the benefit of a chattering monkey.

Softly, Ann drew close. And because the old sailor had such a friendly face, and because she herself was feeling so happy, she dropped suddenly down beside the monkey morsel and cried, "Teach me, too."

"Yessum!" said the old sailor calmly. From the twinkle in his eye Ann felt sure he had heard her very first, sly step. And from his calm tone she realized that news of her coming had been spread by the Wanderer's midnight watchman. "Of course!" said the old sailor. "But first and foremost, introductions. Me, I'm Lumpy. This, she's Ignatz . . ."

"And I, I'm Ann Darrow."

"Kerrect as kin be," declared Lumpy. "And this," he went on, doing bewildering and deft things with his rope, "is a runnin' bowline. Up. Over. And through. Here, you try it."

Ann took the rope, but instead of beginning her lesson she gazed out to the green, gently tumbling sea.

"Oh, Lumpy," she breathed, "isn't it wonderful to be here?"

"Ruther be blowing foam off a tall one in Curly's place any day," Lumpy said frankly, "and I'll betcha Ignatz here'd think the top of a cocoanut tree nineteen times wonderfuller. But everybody to their own taste."

"Oh, of course," Ann conceded, "it won't always be as lovely. I suppose when the sea is rough it's pretty bad."

"It's better," Lumpy admitted dryly, "when you can order the weather. And working hours," he added, rising hastily as a whistle blew.

Warmed to laziness by the sun, Ann kept to her sheltered nook with Ignatz as Lumpy ran off. On the whistle's dying note several other sailors nipped briskly forward while from quarters aft, not far from the companionway by which Ann had got to the deck, came the whistle's owner. This was a young man so intent upon his work that he failed to detect his partly hidden audience of one.

At sight of this young man, Ann's interest in the situation quickened considerably. His long, well-muscled body, his strong dark face, his general air of being master and knowing it, challenged her, but in a fashion which she found not at all unpleasant. This, she decided, would be Driscoll, and as he took a position which presented to her a broad, rakish back, she stood up to secure a better view.

He wore, this Driscoll, an officer's cap and a magnificent black woolen shirt he never could have bought out of a sailor's wage. Otherwise he was dressed not very differently from the men he proceeded to put nimbly to work.

What this work might be was not wholly clear to Ann, except that it had to do with an open hatch, an enormous box some distance away, and what seemed to be a completely baffling tangle of ropes. It was such a complete tangle that Ann moved out a bit in order to watch more easily.

Meanwhile Driscoll continued to issue rapid orders. One sailor let a rope-end fall, and showed no intention of picking it up.

"No! No!" Driscoll shouted. "Carry that line aft!" Backing up to gesture in the proper direction he drew so close to Ann that almost she could have reached out and touched his shoulder. "Aft, aft, you farmer! Back there."

His arm swung back with a full furious sweep, and its finger tips struck stingingly across Ann's face. She staggered to her sun-warmed nook and almost fell. Ignatz broke into a mad chatter.

"Who the . . ." As he wheeled about and sighted Ann, Driscoll checked himself and started over more mildly. "What are you doing up here? You're supposed to be sleeping."

"I just wanted to see," Ann explained. She spoke meekly because she knew the fault had been hers.

"Well, I'm sorry." Driscoll looked sheepishly at his fingers. "I hope the sock didn't land too hard."

"Not at all," Ann cried, so vigorously that they both laughed.

"So!" said Driscoll after a little pause. "You're the girl Denham found at the last minute."

"An awfully excited one at this minute," Ann smiled. "It is all simply bewildering. And I've never been on a ship before."

"And I," replied Driscoll in a change of voice which recalled to Ann that he could be gruff, "have never been on a ship with a woman before."

"I guess you don't think much of a woman on a ship, do you?"

"Not to make any bones about it, she's usually trouble."

"I'll try not to be," Ann said flushing.

"You've got in the way once, already," Driscoll reminded her unsparingly. "Better stay below."

"What? Not the whole voyage?" Ann cried, and had to laugh.

The mate's eyes looked into hers and looked away.

"You can come up once in a while," he granted, struggling to suppress a grin. "Say, does that sock in the jaw hurt any more? It was a dinger."

"I can stand it. Life's been mostly socks in the jaw for me."

Ann's tone was suddenly bitter, and Driscoll looked at her again, more closely.

"If it's been like that," he said, "we'll have to do something about it. I'll tell you. Come up on deck any darn time you please."

Once more their eyes met, and Ann, in faint confusion, bent to pick up the chattering Ignatz, as Denham stepped out of the quarters aft.

"I thought I ordered you to sleep the clock around?" he cried.

"Impossible! I was much too excited to sleep."

"I see you've got acquainted with a couple of the crew already."

"Yes! I find the Mate a little uncontrollable. But Ignatz is peaceable and friendly."

Denham gazed at Ignatz thoughtfully.

"Beauty," he murmured to himself. "Beauty and the Beast!"

"I never claimed to be handsome," Driscoll protested. "But . . ."

"Not you, Jack. Ignatz. See how quiet he has grown. He never was that quiet before, not even in old Lumpy's arms."

"Beauty," Denham repeated to himself after a pause. "Beauty and the Beast. It certainly is interesting. It most certainly is."

"What?" Driscoll asked.

"You'll find out in plenty of time, Jack."

Denham turned to Ann.

"Since you're up, let's find out where we stand. I'll make some screen tests of you. Go down into the cabin. Captain Englehorn will show you the boxes that hold the costumes. Dig out any one that pleases you. By the time you get it on and add some make-up, we'll have plenty of light for the camera."

Ann set Ignatz down.

"Think you know the right make-up for outdoor shots?" Denham asked.

"I think so," Ann said, trying to hide her nervousness. "I won't be long."

When she had gone Driscoll turned to his employer with a little frown.

"She seems like a fine girl."

"I'd swear to that, Jack."

"Not the kind you usually find on a trip like this."

"A lot better."

"I—I wonder if she really ought to be going, Mr. Denham?"

Denham gazed at his mate for a moment in a mixture of puzzled and impatient affection.

"Come along," he said at length. "Help me set up the camera."

They got at this while the crew went about stowing the freight which Driscoll's blow on Ann's face had interrupted. Both pieces of work were finished as Ann came back.

She had found the costume boxes right enough. She wore now a glamorous something different by far from the nondescript dress of her first appearance. A curious primitive something blended of soft rustling grasses and softer, iridescent silken strips. Where it failed to cover her, the flesh of her arms and legs flashed in ivory contrast to the brown of the grasses and the brightness of the cloth.

"She looks like some sort of queer bride," Driscoll muttered.

Denham showed a surprising delight over that impulsive tribute.

"Sure enough?" he asked. "Do you really think so, Jack?"

Driscoll nodded.

"But not the bride of just a plain ordinary man?" Denham pressed him.

"No. Not of . . . not of . . . it sounds insane to say it, but she doesn't seem like the

bride of any man that ever lived . . . of somebody, something else, rather . . ."

"It's my Beauty and the Beast costume," Denham explained with creative pride.

"Whatever it is," Ann came up, "it is the
prettiest costume of the lot."

"Right!" cried Denham. "Stand over there."

"I'm nervous, Mr. Denham. Suppose I don't
photograph to suit you?"

"No chance of that, sister. If I hadn't been
sure of that you wouldn't be aboard. We've got
nothing to worry about but the minor problem
of the best angles."

Ann smiled hopefully, and moved in obedience to her director's gesturing hand. Driscoll,
from a flank, clapped his hands soundlessly to
tell her that in his opinion she had no need to
be concerned. Lumpy and a half dozen sailors
rapidly augmented by another dozen, gathered
attentively in the rear. Ignatz, on Lumpy's shoulder, chipped in a soft interested cry at intervals.
And finally the moustached Englehorn appeared
and from jaws working deliberately over a piece
of plug cut threw Ann a slow, encouraging
smile.

"Profile first!" Denham ordered. He squinted
through the view-finder, threw the camera over
and locked it. "Now! When I start cranking
hold it a minute. Then turn slowly to me. Look
at me. Look surprised. Then smile a little. Then
listen. Then laugh. All right? Camera!"

Ann obeyed. It was easier than she had expected; no different, indeed, than she had done
often at the Fort Lee studio. From behind Denham the sailor's comments began to drift up.

"Don't make much sense to me."

"But ain't she the swell looker?"

"Wonder if he's going to use me in his picture?" Lumpy queried.

"With cameras costing what they do? Not a
chance, Lumpy. He couldn't take the risk."

"That was fine," Denham said, and nodded
permission to relax. "Now I'm going to try a
filter."

"Do you always take the pictures yourself?"
Ann asked as he began expertly to change lenses.

"Ever since my African picture. We were
getting a grand shot of a charging rhino when
the cameraman got scared and bolted. The fat-
head! As if I wasn't right there with a rifle. He
didn't trust me to get the rhino before it got him.
So I haven't fooled with cameramen since. I do
the trick myself."

Englehorn, chewing in a methodical placidity, came over to join Driscoll whose brows were
knit in a faint frown.

"What's the trouble, Jack?"

"He's got me going," the mate replied. "All
this mystery. . . ."

"We've done well enough on two trips," Englehorn reminded him. "He'll bring us through this
one all right."

"But with a woman aboard, it's different."

"That's his business," Englehorn answered indisputably.

"Let's go, Ann!" Denham commanded. "Stand over there. When I start to crank, look up slowly. You're quite calm. Don't expect to see anything. Right? Camera!"

A swift excitement transmitted itself to every watcher as Denham began to turn. He was, for his own part, strung to a tensity which caused his emotions to spill over. And as the scene got under way his face hardened and grew red in his effort to charge Ann with his own mood.

"Look up! Slowly, slowly. You are calm, you see nothing yet. Look higher. Higher. There! Now you see it. You are amazed. You can't believe your own senses. Your eyes open wider. Wider. It's horrible. But you are fascinated. You can't look away. You can't move. What is it? You're helpless, Ann! Not a chance! What can you do? Where can you escape? You're helpless, helpless. But you can scream! There's your one hope. If you can scream! But you can't. Your throat is paralyzed! Try to scream, Ann. Perhaps, if you didn't see, you could do it. If your eyes were turned away. You can't turn them away, but you can cover them, Ann. Throw your arm across your eyes, Ann. And scream! Scream, Ann, for your life!"

Arm across her eyes, and shrinking to smallness in her curiously glamorous dress, Ann screamed. Her wild, high cry swept up and up on the softly blowing wind. It was a scream of true terror. Denham had done what he had hoped to do. Ann was not simulating fear. She was afraid. So truly terror-stricken that in a sympathetic agony Ignatz flung himself around and buried his small head in Lumpy's breast.

"Great!" cried Denham and wiped his beaded forehead. "Sister, you've got what it takes and no mistake."

Driscoll caught Englehorn's shoulder.

"By God!" he whispered, "I've got to know more about this. What is he talking her into? What does he think she is really going to see?"

"Slow speed!" Englehorn whispered back. His jaws never hesitated in their methodical, placid motion. "I guess we can trust him. I guess we've got to trust him."

Chapter 4

The Wanderer's blunt and barnacled nose split the warm, oily expanse with a matter-of-fact precision. Crest after endless foamy crest arose, rolled along her rusty flanks, and was lost in the narrowing wake astern. All waters were alike to the Wanderer. Every last one was made to be split and rolled back along rusty hulls. All you needed was the power to do the splitting and, so far as the Wanderer was concerned, that flowed from her engines with the fidelity of the tides. Those engines throbbed now with no less constancy than when the hull they drove had ploughed the Atlantic at a sweet fourteen knots.

The Atlantic was far astern. The slow drift through the Panama Canal was finished, too, along with the long slide to the Hawaiian Islands, to Japan for more coal, past the Philippines, past Borneo, past even Sumatra. Still the speed was a steady fourteen.

The direction was south and west. The time was mid-day. The weather was hot. It was so hot that the crew wore only such garments as the presence of a lady commanded. Some wore hardly that much. Lumpy, sprawling in the shade alongside an inert Ignatz, was as naked as a Sioux down to his waist. There was nothing, not even an excess of flesh, to keep an interested anatomist from counting every one of his hard, thin ribs. From his waist hung a pair of frayed trousers that stopped halfway between his sharp old knees and his sharper ankles. And, on his own word, that was everything . . . to the last patch and thread.

It was a costume admirably suited to the temperature. And yet the temperature might have been hotter, considering that the Wanderer ploughed the sultry latitudes of the Indian Ocean. The Wanderer's first mate, in ducks and a pongee shirt, was fairly cool. At least he would have been if he had not worked up a warm impatience over the failure of an expected figure to appear.

Ann did appear at last. She was wearing white, too, a soft linen sun hat, a stiffly starched linen dress, canvas shoes, but no more stockings than Lumpy himself. Her rounded ankles were

shaded as golden as autumn leaves. And sun-
burn laid a rosy shadow upon her cheeks.

"Good afternoon, Lumpy," she called.

Lumpy sat up, and rubbed his sun-kissed ribs,
and made Ignatz sit up also, to bow.

"And what about me?" Driscoll protested.

"Hello, Jack," Ann smiled.

"Where have you been so long?"

"Trying on more costumes for Mr. Denham."
She nodded with open satisfaction. "And I
looked very nice in them, too."

"Why not give me a chance to see?"

"You? You've had chances galore! All the
times Mr. Denham has had me out here on deck,
making tests."

"All the times! Once or twice."

"Dozens of times."

Driscoll shook his head pityingly.

"Some people need a lot of convincing before
they can make up their minds."

"It's very important to find out which side of
my face photographs best."

"What's wrong with either side?"

"Probably Mr. Denham has found a hundred
terrible faults."

"Both sides look good to me."

Ann beckoned to Ignatz and that eager play-
mate leaped into her arms. From behind the
partial concealment he offered she smiled a
little shyly.

"Yes, but you aren't my movie director."

"If I were," Driscoll said, turning solemn, "you wouldn't be here."

"Well! That's a nice thing to say."

"You know what I mean, Ann!" He maintained solemnity in spite of her beguiling eyes. "It's fine to have you on the ship, of course. But what are you here for? What crazy show is Denham planning to put you through when we get to . . . wherever we're going?"

"I don't care what he is planning. I don't even mind that he is keeping secret where we are going. No matter where we go; no matter what he asks me to do, I've had this." She waved a slim arm to take in all that was visible from the Wanderer's stern to her prow. "I've had the happiest time of my life on this old ship."

"Do you mean that, Ann?"

"Of course!" But she fled at once into smiling generalities. "Everyone's so nice. Lumpy, and you. Mr. Denham and the Skipper. Isn't the Captain a sweet old lamb?"

"A what?" Driscoll looked around in dismay lest the crew had heard; or worse, the Skipper himself.

"I said a sweet old lamb."

"What a row there'd be," Driscoll cried, "if he heard anyone but you say so!"

They strolled to the railing and looked idly down upon the tropical sea. The water flashed with countless tiny specks which closer inspection revealed as small jellyfish, each with its miniature upright sail. No, one was too large to fit easily into the palm of a hand, but there they were, confidently a-sail in the middle of the ocean. Sea asters, Lumpy called them.

Ann and Driscoll were contentedly silent. In the weeks which had elapsed since the Wanderer left New York, they had come surprisingly close. Driscoll was reticent, and unused to girls; yet he had told Ann about his running away to sea to escape going to college. He had told her of his mother, who had forgiven him and who had braced herself to all his dangerous adventures since his meeting with Denham. Ann had told Driscoll, and only Driscoll, of the past which had led up to the miracle-working apple. She had told him of her ranch home, of the loss of her father and mother, of the treachery of the uncle to whom she had confided her inheritance after her father's death. She had told him of her coming to New York, of the despairing quest for work, of her hunger and fear.

Her thoughts were running on that now.

"I was lucky," she said suddenly, soberly, "to have Mr. Denham run across me that night in New York."

"Speaking of Denham, may he cut in?" asked a brisk voice behind them and they turned to see the moving picture director rocking on speculative heels.

"More tests?" Driscoll wanted to know.

Ann expectantly handed Ignatz back to Lumpy, but Denham shook his head.

"Nothing to rush about," he said, "but when you aren't busy, Ann, you might do a bit of sewing. I noticed just now that the Beauty and the Beast costume was ripped along the lining. And above everything else, I want that piece all ready when we need it."

"I'll mend it right away," Ann promised. "It must have got torn when I took it off yesterday."

As she disappeared, Denham lighted a cigarette. He offered one to Driscoll, but the first mate shoved his hands deep into his pockets, doubling them there so that they stood out in hard, distinct lumps beneath the white cloth.

"Mr. Denham," he said doggedly, "I'm going to do some butting in."

"What's on your mind, Jack?" Denham asked, and considered the smoking tip of his cigarette.

"When do we find out where we're going?"

"Pretty soon now." Denham smiled.

"Are you going to tell us what happens when we get there?"

"Don't ask me to play fortune teller, young fella."

"But damn it! You must have some idea what you're after."

Denham snapped his cigarette over the side and eyed Driscoll questioningly:

"Going soft on me, Jack?"

"You know I'm not."

"Then why all the fuss and blow?"

"You know it isn't for myself. It's Ann . . ."

"Oh!" Denham grew coolly serious. "So you've already gone soft on her. Better cut that out, Jack. I've got enough on my hands. Don't pile on a love affair to complicate things more."

"Who said anything about a love affair?" Driscoll flushed.

"It never fails," Denham said, looking thoughtfully up toward the crow's nest. "Some big, hardboiled egg meets up with a pretty face, and bingo! He cracks up and melts."

"Who's cracking up?" Driscoll demanded indignantly. "I haven't run out on you, have I?"

"No-o-o! And I've always figured you for a good tough guy, Jack. But if Beauty gets you . . ." He caught himself and laughed a little. "Why, I'm almost into my theme song."

"What in blazes are you talking about?"

"It's the idea I'm building my picture on, Jack. The Beast was a tough guy, tougher than you or anybody ever written about. He could lick the world. But when Beauty came along, she got him. When he saw her, he went soft. He forgot his code. And the little ham-and-egg fighters slapped him down. Think that over, young fella."

Driscoll was still staring in angry puzzlement at his smiling employer when a young sailor hurried up.

"Mr. Denham," he said. "The Skipper says,

will you please come up on the bridge? We've reached the position you marked, he says."

"Right, Jimmy."

Denham's face lighted, and he squared his shoulders in the characteristic gesture of triumph which had marked him in the moment of his discovery of Ann.

"Come on, Jack. You're in on this. You wanted to know where we were going. Follow me. I'm going to spill it."

He raced off to the bridge, and Driscoll, with eyes bright, made a close second.

Captain Englehorn, placid, methodical, even in this moment of long-awaited revelation, was looking down upon a table which held an outspread chart.

"Here's our noon position," he said, between slow chews. "Two South, ninety East. You promised me some information, Mr. Denham, at this point."

"'Way west of Sumatra." Denham looked tensely down at the chart. "That's right! 'Way west of Sumatra."

"'Way out of any waters I know," said Englehorn. "I can read the East Indies like my own hand. But I was never around this place before."

"Where do we go from here?" Driscoll asked eagerly.

"South-west," Denham snapped.

"South-west?" Englehorn chewed more slowly. "But in that direction there is nothing . . .

nothing for thousands of miles. What about food? So many in the crew makes the food go fast. And water? And coal?"

"Ease off, Skipper." Denham laughed, his shoulders still square, his face alight. "We're not going much more than around the corner from here."

He took a wallet from his breast pocket, opened it, drew out a heavy envelope and from its protecting thickness produced two well worn pieces of paper. These he spread out upon the table under the eyes of his captain and mate.

"There's the island we're looking for."

"Ah! The position of it." Englehorn leaned over the chart, and then straightened up. "Mr. Driscoll, fetch the big chart."

"You won't find that island on any chart, big or little, Skipper. All we've got to go by I've shown you here. This picture and the position, both made up by a friend of mine, the skipper of a Norwegian barque."

"He was kidding," Driscoll said.

"Listen!" Denham faced the other two as though he would convince them by eye as well as by tongue. "A canoe with natives from this island was blown out to sea. When my Norwegian barque picked them up only one was alive. He died before they reached port; but not before his story had enabled the skipper to piece together a description of the island and a fairly good idea of where it lies."

"And where did you come in?" Driscoll asked, while Englehorn chewed methodically.

"Two years ago, in Singapore. I'd known the Norwegian for years. He was sure I'd be interested."

"Does he believe the native's story, this Norwegian?" Englehorn murmured.

"Who cares? I do! Why shouldn't I? Do you think a picture as detailed as that could grow entirely out of the imagination?"

The map was, in truth, impressive. It began, at the left, with a long, sandy peninsula, a mile or more in extent. In front of the peninsula a reef was indicated, with a tortuous passageway sketchily outlined. In the other direction the peninsula's sparsely wooded extent ended abruptly against a steep precipice. This precipice, according to the Norwegian skipper's rough notes, was hundreds of feet high and marked the edge of a dense growth which covered the many square miles comprising the rest of the island. Above the dense upland growth, and seemingly from the center of it, rose a mountain whose crudely drawn outline suggested a skull. The last detail was the most curious, and startling. It was a wall, higher than a dozen tall men, and impregnable. And this wall, at the base of the peninsula, stretched from the sea on one side to the sea on the other, serving as a mighty barrier against who or what might attempt to come down the precipice from the back country.

"A wall!" Englehorn murmured.

"And what a wall!" Denham said. "Built so long ago that the descendants of the builders have slipped back into savagery, and have completely forgotten the remarkable civilization which erected the shield on which they now depend. But the wall is as strong today as it was ages ago."

Denham paused to nod emphatically.

"The natives take care that it never grows weak. They need it."

"Why?" Driscoll wanted to know.

"Because there's something on the other side . . . something they fear."

"A tribe of enemies, I guess," Englehorn murmured.

Denham looked sidewise at his skipper, his brown eyes snapping; then sat down and reached for his seldom unemployed package of cigarettes.

"Did either of you ever hear," he asked, "of . . . Kong?"

Driscoll shook his head. Englehorn chewed thoughtfully.

"Kong? Why . . . yes. A Malay superstition. Is not that it? A God, or devil, or something?"

"Something, all right," Denham agreed. "But neither man nor beast. Something monstrous.

All powerful. Terribly alive. Holding that island in the grip of deadly fear, as it held those intelligent ancestors who built the mighty wall."

Englehorn resumed his placid, methodical chewing. Driscoll was plainly skeptical.

"I tell you there's something on that island," Denham declared. "Something no white man has ever seen. Every legend has a basis of truth."

"And," exclaimed Englehorn in tardy enlightenment, "you expect to photograph it."

"Whatever is there. You bet I'll photograph it."

"Suppose," Driscoll suggested, dryly, "that it doesn't like to have its picture taken?"

Denham stood up smiling, and dusted his hands in brisk good cheer.

"Suppose it doesn't?" he said. "Why do you suppose I brought those gas bombs?"

He turned and stared into the southwest. Skeptical though he was and anxious for Ann, Driscoll could not resist staring too, and in spite of himself, his eyes sparkled with a reckless excitement. Englehorn, chewing placidly, considered the pictured island and then taking a pair of dividers, he began locating it upon the chart outspread upon his table.

Chapter 5

High above the Wanderer's scorched and peeling deck, Driscoll pushed up the floor plate of the crow's nest and clambered through. Once on his feet he reached down to Ann. His brown hand closed over her slight wrist with careful deliberation. When she had got in, the trap dropped beneath his feet and the pair of them swayed slowly in cadence with the gently rocking mast.

So high up, they could feel a little wind, and Ann pushed her yellow hair severely back over small shapely ears that every available bit of face and neck might receive the welcome breeze. Driscoll nodded approval as he wiped his damp forehead.

From their high perch the ocean seemed even more brilliantly blue than it had been from the ship's side. Miles to the south a something resembling a fleecy rope stretched along the water, its ends disappearing in distance which baffled the eye. It seemed no higher than a hand's breadth, but at intervals it swelled a little and threw off wispy tendrils.

Against the blue sweep of the sky there showed only one bit of life. An albatross moved far off and close to the line where sea and sky met. It curved and swung like a brilliantly maneuvered aeroplane between them and the late afternoon sun.

"How splendid!" cried Ann. "Why didn't you bring me up here before? I feel like an explorer."

"Let's see," Driscoll considered, grinning. "An explorer is someone who gets there first. Well, you're an explorer then, sure enough. You're the first woman ever to set foot in this crow's nest."

"And going to an island where we'll *all* be the first white people. It's terribly exciting. When do you think we'll get there?" Ann lifted an eager questioning face.

"Well, if there is any such place," Driscoll answered, smiling down at her indulgently, "we ought to find it in the next twenty-four hours."

"Mr. Denham's so worked up about it he can't

keep still. I don't believe he went to bed all last night."

"I'm kind of worked up myself," Driscoll admitted, looking toward the southwest.

Ann turned upon him accusingly.

"You? Why, you don't even believe there *is* an island."

"I hope there isn't," Driscoll said soberly.

"And you the lad who ran away from home to find a life of adventure! Fie, Mr. Mate!"

Her voice was teasing. If she had any suspicion as to the cause of his reluctance to encounter Mystery Island, she did not betray it. Driscoll looked at her sharply.

"Don't you know why I'm worked up, Ann? Don't you know it's because of you? Denham's such a fool for risks. What will he expect you to do?"

"After what he did for me, Jack, I'd do whatever he asks. You wouldn't want me to do anything else."

"Yes I would, Ann. There's a right limit. But Denham doesn't remember it when there's a picture at stake. He doesn't care what happens, so long as he gets what he's after. Yes, I know! You're going to say that he never asks us to do what he won't do, and that's o. k. as far as men are concerned. But it's different with you aboard."

"Well, you don't need to worry yet."

"I can't help it. If anything happened to you. . . ! Ann, look at me!"

Instead of looking, Ann turned her head so that only one white ear with a wisp of yellow curl behind it remained in Driscoll's view.

"Ann, you know I love you!"

Still, she did not turn her head, but the ear with the curl behind it grew pink.

Driscoll put his hands on her shoulders, drew her slowly against him.

For the briefest moment, Ann rested there. Then she twisted away to welcome a chattering Ignatz who appeared behind them.

"Jack! He's broken loose again."

"Ann! Look at me!"

But Ann was too busy with the wildly careening Ignatz. He leaped to her shoulder and clung about her neck.

"I really believe he's jealous of you, Jack."

Driscoll lifted the monkey ungently and firmly from her neck.

"Ann!" he said. "We have so little time. Please, Ann, I'm scared *of* you, and I'm scared *for* you, and I love you so."

Ann looked at him then, and with an end to all pretense she stepped forward into his arms. Driscoll's lips bent to her hair, to the ear with the curl behind it, to her lips which she lifted, curving them into a smile.

Sunset had come on. The bright clear blue of the daylight sky was flooded to the westward with pinks and indigos, with emeralds and jades, with russet, saffron, peach and yellow.

Against this brilliant camouflage, the distant albatross swung briefly and was lost to sight.

Southward the faint fleecy rope had grown by minute degrees to a low barrier of fog which was moving perceptibly closer to the ship.

None on the crow's nest noticed it, however; least of all, Ignatz, who chattered furiously at Ann's feet.

Chapter 6

All through the night the fog thickened. Hours before daylight the Wanderer, headed by Captain Englehorn toward the Norwegian skipper's incredible island, had slowed to little more than steerage way. When morning came she was still creeping through a yellow-white blanket, miles in extent.

Against the penetrating dampness of this blanket no garment was proof. The clothes of everyone drooped in loose, sodden folds. Water dripped everywhere, from spars, stays and walls, and gathering on the cold deck ran in slow, uncertain rivulets.

At a distance of a dozen feet, men and such solid objects as masts and ventilators became vaguely wavering wraiths. At greater distances they vanished behind the soft, yellow-white silence. Up on the bridge Denham and Englehorn, Driscoll and Ann could see nothing of the sailor who heaved a lead in the bow, or of the other sailor who tried to pierce the thick veil from the high vantage point of the crow's nest. These could be heard, however. By some atmospheric trick their voices seemed to ring more loudly through the fog than they had ever come through clear sunlight.

"This triple-damned fog!" Denham choked. He could scarcely speak from excitement. He was as tense as a man on a tight rope, and he never stopped staring forward into the enwrapping cloud. "Are you sure of your position, Skipper?"

"Sure!" Englehorn murmured placidly, and cut himself some fresh plug cut. "Last night, before this stuff closed around us, I got a fine sight."

"Jack!" Ann whispered, taking a fresh hold on Driscoll's hand. "If we don't get somewhere soon, I'll explode. I never was so excited in my life."

"Don't bounce around so," Driscoll warned her. "Next thing you know you'll be rolling off the ship. And don't," he added more soberly, "keep doing things to get *me* excited. I'm fit to be tied right now. I'd like to throw my cap up into the air and yell Blue Blazes. But when I think of what we may be taking you into, I know I've got to keep my head."

"If your position is right, Skipper," said Denham, "we ought to be near the island."

"If we don't see it when this fog lifts," Englehorn murmured confidently, "we never shall. We've quartered these parts. Either we're on top of it or we've found blue water in the place it should be."

The high, intent voice of the sailor in the bow came sharply up to the bridge.

"No bottom at thirty fathoms."

"Of course," Driscoll ventured, almost hopefully, "that Norse skipper was just guessing at the position."

"How will we know it's the right island?" Ann asked.

"I told you!" Denham rasped impatiently. "The mountain!" His eyes tried to pierce the fog. "The mountain that looks like a skull."

"I'd forgotten," Ann apologized. "Of course. Skull Mountain."

"Bottom!" The high voice shot back from the bow, and at that triumphant cry they all stiffened. "Bottom! Twenty fathoms!"

"I knew it." Englehorn chewed placidly. "She's shallowing fast. Dead slow, Mr. Driscoll. Tell 'em!"

Driscoll tore into the wheel house and spoke

down the engine room tube. Bells jangled below in reply and the Wanderer dropped off to a speed that was scarcely more than drifting.

"Look!" Ann cried. "Isn't the fog thinner?"

"Sixteen!" came the voice from the bow. "Sixteen fathoms!"

"What does she draw, Skipper?" Denham demanded.

"Six!" For the first time, Englehorn was stirred out of his customary placidity. He was like Denham now, staring intently, listening even more intently.

"Listen!" Ann whispered.

"What do you hear?" Denham whispered back.

Ann shook her head, and with the other three continued to listen. Suddenly the young, nervous voice of Jimmy dropped down from the crow's nest.

"Breakers!"

"Where away?" Driscoll shouted.

"Dead ahead!"

Driscoll leaped for the wheel house and the engine room tube again. His order came out to the others sharp and clear, and its dying note was followed by the jangle of the engine room's bells and the roll and thunder of the Wanderer's reversing engines.

"Ten fathoms!" called the man in the bow.

"Let go!" Englehorn roared mightily.

Up forward dim wraiths leaped to action. A

chain clanked and rattled through a hawse
pipe. An anchor splashed. More bells jangled
below. The Wanderer was suddenly motionless and still. Everyone listened.

"That's not breakers," Driscoll declared
roundly.

"It's drums," Englehorn murmured, placid
once more.

The fog, which had been thinning almost
imperceptibly, lifted while they listened. Before the edge of a brisk, sheering wind it
parted and rolled away. The blue sea lay exposed under a sun but faintly veiled. And a
little way off, hardly more than a quarter of a
mile, a high wooded island with a skull-like
knob reached out toward the ship with a long,
brush-covered finger of sand and rocks.

"Skull Mountain!" Denham flung out a victorious arm. "Do you see it? And the wall! The
wall! The wall!" He struck Englehorn's back
a mighty blow. "There it is. Do you believe
me now?" Just short of hysteria he half
climbed, half slid down from the bridge and
raced toward the bow of the ship. "Get out
the boats!" he shouted back. "Get out the
boats!"

"Jack!" cried Ann. "Did you ever see anything like it? Isn't it wonderful?"

All the excitement drained out of Driscoll
as he looked down at her face. His mouth
tightened somberly. He strode forward to

direct the lowering of the boats and the stowing of equipment.

After a little, Denham came rushing back to
where the crew were loading the boats, and
Ann went down to him.

"I'm going ashore with you, aren't I?" she
asked.

"You bet!"

Driscoll, overhearing, left his work promptly.

"Ought she to quit the ship before we find
out what's going on . . . what we're likely to
run into?"

"Look here, Jack!" Denham complained
cheerfully. "Who's running this show? I've
learned by bitter experience to keep my cast
and my cameras all together and right with
me. How do I know when I'll want 'em?"

"But Mr. Denham!" Driscoll half turned
from Ann, to keep her from hearing. "It's
crazy to risk. . . ."

"Get back to work, Jack," Denham directed
bluntly. "Go on! Deal out rifles and ammunition. See that a dozen of the gas bombs are
taken. And pick me a couple of huskies to
carry my picture stuff."

Driscoll wavered, and then with a helpless
shrug and a last frown in Ann's direction
turned to his sailors. Denham shook his head
in amiable exasperation and winked at Ann.

"Have somebody get the costume box up

and into one of the boats," he said. "If we're lucky we may get a swell shot right away."

As Ann went below, Denham mounted to the bridge. There Englehorn was sweeping the island with his binoculars.

"See anything, Skipper?"

"Nothing but those few huts at the edge of the brush on the peninsula."

"I took a look from the bow, and I think there are more and bigger houses back in the thicker brush."

"It's the first native island I ever called at where the whole tribe didn't come down to the beach for a look-see."

"The tribe is somewhere, sure enough. Hear those drums?"

Englehorn nodded and both men listened. A deep, soft clamor rolled across the intervening water, and slowly resolved itself into a swift, importunate rhythm.

"Funny they haven't spotted us," Denham said.

"Every last native ought to be out and down at the water's edge," Englehorn insisted.

"Maybe they *have* seen us, and are signaling."

"You've heard native drums before, Mr. Denham," Englehorn demurred calmly. "You know those ain't signal beats. There's some ceremony inland. A big ceremony, too, if you ask me."

He descended from the bridge and walked quietly over to where by now Driscoll had practically completed the work of lowering the boats and loading them. He watched for a space and then looked toward the forward deck.

"Fetch the boatswain," he commanded.

That petty officer, a thick, heavy sailorman, hurried up.

"This man will stay aboard with fourteen sailors," Englehorn said to Driscoll. "You choose the fourteen. All the others will go ashore with us."

Driscoll nodded soberly and went about the selection. He chose Lumpy first of all, to that veteran adventurer's audible chagrin.

"Who'll be in charge of my gas bombs?" Denham wanted to know.

"You take 'em, Jimmy," Driscoll ordered.

Jimmy stooped over the box, hefted it experimentally, looked slightly injured at the weight of it, and then bore his burden over to the last boat.

"Of course you're coming, Skipper?" Denham asked.

"Got to keep my record clear," Englehorn nodded. "Never yet missed looking over a native island once I caught up with it."

"You're likely to be a big help. You'll probably have to do the talking. Their lingo isn't likely to be one I've picked up."

"All right," Driscoll said. "Both boats are ready."

Englehorn and Denham climbed down into the first one, and at the order of the former the crew pushed off. Driscoll motioned the second boat to wait where it swung on its davits. Ann was hurrying across the deck. He helped her in silently, then directed that the boat be lowered. While it settled into the water he took a last look around deck.

"Better serve out rifles and ammunition," he said to the boatswain. "And it wouldn't hurt to do some figuring on the range from here to the island."

With a last look, he swung over the side and joined Ann.

"This is the first time I ever saw the whole crew together," Ann said. "I hadn't realized it was so large."

"Twenty men in each boat," Driscoll told her. "And," he added gloomily, "we'll need 'em."

"Nonsense! Probably the natives will be as friendly as reservation Indians."

"More probably not. Hear those drums? I overheard the Skipper tell Denham they were beating up some kind of ceremony. I wish I knew what kind."

"Maybe they're announcing some pretty girl's engagement."

Driscoll looked at her. Her yellow hair was

bare to the sun and blowing about her flushed excited face.

"Speaking of pretty girls' engagements," he said, and looked back up at the crow's nest.

But the drums grew louder with every tug of the boat's oars; the rhythm grew more distinct; and as Englehorn had said, it sounded too majestic to be a mere signal. Driscoll's momentary elation left him.

Englehorn's boat had reached the beach and Denham was already ashore, putting his camera on its tripod. While Driscoll's crew spurted through the surf the producer burdened one sailor with the mounted machine, another with a case of films, and a third with a box containing costumes. Meanwhile Englehorn was dividing cases of trade goods among the others. Jimmy, showing his grievance in every line of his young face, shouldered the heavy container which held the gas bombs.

"You stick close to me, Jimmy," Denham directed. "And watch your step. There's enough trichloride in that case to put a herd of hippos to sleep."

"Are we going to see any hippos?" Jimmy wanted to know.

"Something a lot more exciting, I hope. Where's Driscoll?"

Driscoll came trotting over, followed by Ann. His boat was beached alongside the other.

"Leave an armed man in charge of each boat."

"All attended to."

"Stay by me, Ann."

"I'll look after Ann," Driscoll announced quickly.

Denham chuckled. The wild excitement of those moments preceding the sighting of the island was gone. He was once more solid, indomitable, and quick with a characteristic tolerance.

"All right, Jack. All set, Skipper?"

Englehorn nodded. He and Driscoll signalled, and the two boat crews fell into a loose double column. Denham, already striding vigorously toward the scattered houses visible at the edge of the brush, automatically became the head of the line of march. Behind him paced the men bearing camera and films, then Englehorn, then Driscoll and Ann.

As the party sloped up from the water line and achieved some small elevation the wall began to bulk large, although still far off. It was enormous. The Norwegian skipper's crude sketch had poorly estimated the mighty barrier which ran the full extent of the peninsula. Brush closed in upon its base. There were even occasional intervening trees. But all growth stopped far below the rampart's top. Its vastness was not dwarfed even by the overhanging precipice. It was made chiefly of huge logs. At one point, however, there seemed to be a gate hinged to massive stone pillars supporting the story of the structure's antiquity.

The cadenced drum beats grew louder as the Wanderer's party approached, but no living persons were seen in the straggling huts first met up with. None appeared even when the explorers were past the outskirts of the village. The size of this indicated a tribe of several hundred members, filling an area of six or eight city blocks. The houses were all large, and quite widely separated. Each was enclosed and partially masked by the thick brush. Narrow paths through the undergrowth were the only connecting links. Each stood otherwise by itself in the center of a bare circle beaten to dusty surface smoothness by many feet. One extraordinary detail made the village different from any which either Englehorn or Denham had ever seen. This was the scattering of magnificent, broken columns of carved stone, and fragments of skillfully built walls. These stood on every hand, but the majority were forward, closer to the wall.

"My guess," said Denham pointing to the barrier, "is that it must once have been the outer defence of a sizeable city. Isn't it enormous?"

"Colossal," Englehorn agreed.

"It's almost Egyptian," Denham mused.

"Who do you suppose could have built it?" Ann asked in an awed tone.

"I went up to Angkor once," Driscoll remarked in solemn admiration. "That's bigger than this. Nobody knows who built it, either."

"What a chance!" Denham exulted. "What a picture!"

Still no one was sighted. But suddenly between two steps, the roll of the drums softened. And now, above their low, purring note, voices rose in a wildly swelling chant. Driscoll halted and flung up an arm in warning. Ann clutched Driscoll's sleeve and the sailors looked at one another apprehensively. The sound of the chant came from somewhere close to the wall. Denham motioned to Englehorn, and pointed to an unusually large house ahead.

"If we get around that," he said, "I'll bet we will see them."

"Do you hear what they're saying?" Ann whispered to Driscoll. "They're shouting, 'Kong! Kong!'"

"Denham!" Driscoll called. "Do you catch that? They're at some god ceremony."

"I hear!" Denham said. "Come on."

Moving forward cautiously, he beckoned Englehorn closer.

"Think you can speak their lingo?"

"Can't catch any words yet." Englehorn listened acutely. "It does, though, sound a bit like the talk of the Nias Islanders."

"What luck if it is enough alike," Denham laughed.

They were directly at the masking house now, and Denham halted, waving the rest of the column to close up and gather near. He, himself advanced, guardedly, to the corner of the house.

"Easy now!" he whispered. "Stay here till I see what is going on!"

He disappeared while Driscoll, with Ann keeping close, eyed his men to measure their degree of readiness and Englehorn bit off another half inch of plug cut. He came back with his eyes blazing.

"Holy mackerel!" he whispered. "Englehorn! Driscoll! Get a look at this thing. But be quiet."

Himself so eager for quiet that he moved upon tiptoes, he motioned to the camera bearer, took over the machine and tripod, and slowly began to work it around the corner of the house.

While he maneuvered, the drums rolled softly. Above their murmurous rhythm the explosive shout of many voices rose like thunder. Ecstatic. Triumphant. Awed. Fearful. All these emotions were conveyed by turns. Irre-

sistibly drawn, the sailors and Ann drifted
slowly forward until, standing clear of the
masking house, they looked upon the chanting host.

Chapter 7

In front of them lay a great, beaten square which ended only at the wall. Frowning down upon this square, stood the tremendous gate, sighted dimly back on the beach. Up to the gate's sill rose a series of broad, stone steps; and half-way up the steps, on a rude dais covered with skins, knelt a young native girl. There could not have been found in any tribe many maidens as smoothly attractive as she, and the woven strands of flowers, which served as crown, girdle and necklace and her only apparel, increased her soft, frightened charm. On either side of the girl, some on the stairs, some in the square, the chanting natives swayed in ordered ranks. A little to one side, but dominating the scene by eye and gesture, a wizened, coal-black witch doctor pranced in a solemn ritualistic dance. Still farther to one side a veritable giant, magnificently costumed in furs, grass and feathers, watched with a kingly detachment. To the last one, men, women, children, witch doctor and king, all were so wrapped up in the ceremony that none noticed the newly arrived audience.

"Oh, Lord!" Denham whispered. "Make 'em hold it!" and he began to crank his camera.

"What's that old guy in the feathered dress doing?" Jimmy asked under his breath.

Very close to the flower-dressed girl, the witch doctor began an oddly supplicating gyration. His hands, in slow, humble gestures, seemed to offer the maiden to a dozen huge dancers who leaped out of the chanting ranks; a terrifying dozen, whose heads were concealed by hollowed, furry skulls, and whose bodies were hidden by rough, black skins.

"Gorillas!" Englehorn murmured thoughtfully. "Those men are playing at being gorillas, or something like. They're acting out a ritual. . . ."

He looked suddenly back at Ann, and then moved to put his lean figure more squarely between her and the natives. Moved by a seemingly common impulse the Wanderer's whole crew jostled more closely together, until Ann had to push some of them aside, and stand on tiptoe. Even then she was well concealed.

As the gigantic apelike beings advanced, the witch doctor moved back and looked toward the king. It was, plainly, his majesty's time to enter the ceremony. What his part was, the watchers were not to know until long after, for as he shifted his position the corner of one eye took in Denham at the camera, and then the whole party of watchers.

"Bado!" he shouted and wheeled to face them. "Bado! Dama pati vego!"

The chanting, the dancing, all sound, all movement turned into a dead stony silence. In the midst of this Englehorn's placid, practical voice went forward to Denham.

"There's luck," he murmured. "I can understand his lingo. He's telling the old witch doctor to stop, to 'ware strangers."

All the natives had turned and were staring; and as though an order had come to them out of the silence the women and children began to slip away.

"Look!" Jimmy said. "Their women are clearing out. We'd better beat it or we'll be up to our necks in trouble."

He whirled around, to start for the beach, but Driscoll seized his arm.

"Good catch, Jack!" Denham called from his forward position as spearpoint of the party.

"No use trying to hide now. Everybody stand fast. Put up a bold front."

The gigantic king, after a full stare, made up his mind. His great arm beckoned two warriors only a little smaller than himself, and so guarded he moved slowly forward. The last of the women and children vanished.

"Mr. Denham!" Jimmy cried. "What's the big bozo up to?"

"Shut up!" Denham answered, without taking his eyes off the king. "I don't know."

The chief took another slow, majestic stride.

"Jack!" whispered Ann. "Does it mean trouble when the women and children go away?"

"Trouble for those blacks if they start anything," Jack assured her and laughed briskly.

The chief continued to advance. Some of the sailors shifted their rifles, and their fingers sought the triggers. Denham, as though he had eyes in the back of his head, called a warning.

"Steady, boys! There's nothing to get nervous about!"

"And that's the truth," Jack told Ann cheerfully. "It's all bluff so far. The chief's waiting to see if we'll scare. It's all a game of bluff, and I'm betting on us."

The chief stopped a half dozen paces in front of Denham and waited.

"Come on, Skipper," the producer called.

"If you can talk his lingo, make a friendly speech."

Englehorn started to move closer, but the chief flung up an arresting hand.

"Watu! Tama di? Tama di?"

"Greetings!" Englehorn replied slowly. "We are your friends. Bala! Bala! Friends! Friends!"

"Bali, reri!" the king shouted scornfully. "Tasko! Tasko!"

"What's he say, Skipper?" Denham asked out of a corner of his mouth.

"Says he wants no friends. Tells us to beat it!"

"Talk him out of it," Denham ordered. "Ask him what the ceremony is."

Englehorn spoke in placid, conciliating tones and pointed to the flower-dressed girl.

"Ani saba Kong!" said the king doubtfully; and from all the natives came a sighing, worshipful murmur. "Saba Kong!"

"He says the girl is the bride of Kong."

"Kong!" Denham cried exultantly. "Didn't I tell you?"

Before either king or interpreter could speak again, the witch doctor suddenly leaped forward, his headdress shaking, his eyes darting fury at both king and strangers.

"Dama si vego!" he screamed. His old, frail voice ran on like a discordant violin note. "Dama si vego. Punya. Punya bas!"

"What's up now?" Denham demanded.

"He says the ceremony's spoiled because we've seen it."

"Let me get at him," Denham said confidently. "What's the word for 'friend'?"

"Bala."

Denham squared his shoulders and spread out his hands, taking a smiling, conciliatory step.

"Bala!" he said. "Bala! Bala!" He pointed to himself and then to the king and the witch doctor. "Bala! Bala! Bala!"

The king hesitated but the old sorcerer had not the faintest doubt of his proper course. His frown was as deep as Denham's smile was wide. His hand beckoned the warriors up from the rear.

"Tasko!" he screamed. The king, taking his cue, roared, "Tasko!" The two guards beside him swung their spears up to a position of ready. The massed warriors behind began to surge forward.

Excitement overcoming fright, Ann balanced herself against Driscoll and rose high on her tiptoes to see. Her foaming, honey-colored hair caught the sun and the king's eye in the same instant. He ceased his shout as though his mouth had been clamped shut and stared, first at Ann and then at the witch doctor, as though for confirmation.

"Malem ma pakeno!" he stammered. "Sita!"

He jerked his arm at the witch doctor. "Malem! Malem ma pakeno!"

The witch doctor, his cries also ceasing, stared too. The warriors stopped stock still and their weapon points fell.

"Now what?" Denham asked with a little gesture of relief.

"He said," Englehorn explained, "Look! The woman of gold!"

"Blondes are scarce around here," Denham chuckled.

The king's voice rose ecstatically, "Kong! Malem ma pakeno! Kong wa bisa! Kow bisa para Kong," and he turned to the witch doctor seeking agreement.

The old sorcerer nodded thoughtfully as Englehorn translated swiftly.

"The woman of gold. Kong's gift. A gift for Kong."

"Good Lord!" Denham protested.

The king and the witch doctor advanced upon Denham and the former thrust out his arm in a regal command.

"Dama!" he said. "Tebo malem na hi!"

"Stranger! Sell the woman to us." Englehorn's translation followed like pistol cracks, and his eyes asked what Denham proposed to do.

"Dia malem!" the king hurried on.

"Six women!" Englehorn said swiftly. "He will give six for yours of gold."

Ann gasped and tried to smile.

"You got Ann into this, Denham!" Driscoll cried. "What's our cue?"

Denham smiled briefly, and with an unhurried gesture called up his two carriers.

"Tell him, as politely as you can," he said to Englehorn, "that we'd rather not swap." Out of a corner of his mouth he added, to Ann, "This isn't my trading day, sister."

"Tida!" Englehorn murmured to the king in sorrow-stricken tones. "No! Malem ati rota na ni! Our woman is our luck and we dare not part with her."

Against that refusal, bland though it had been, the witch doctor cried in fury. "Watu!" he screamed. "Tam bisa para Kong di wana ta!"

"They can't lose Kong's gift."

"That's enough for me," Driscoll growled, as Englehorn tossed back the swift interpretation, "I'm taking Ann back to the ship."

"We'd all better slide out," Englehorn warned Denham casually, "before that smart old witch doctor thinks to send out a war party to get between us and our boats."

"I suppose so!" Denham spoke reluctantly, not wanting to lose any chance for a good scene for his movie. "But don't let's leave the old coot so mad, Skipper. Tell him we'll be back tomorrow to make friends and talk things over."

"Dulu!" Englehorn promised the chief and

witch doctor gently. And the promise made cover for the quick retreat of the men who bore the camera and the tripod. "Tomorrow! Hi tego nah! We return then."

"En Malem?" the chief insisted. "Malem ma pakeno?"

"The woman of gold?"

"Get going!" Denham ordered briskly to the crew. "And keep smiling, Ann. Don't you realize the chief's just paid you a whopping compliment? Six for one! Smile at Jack. And keep your chin up."

"Dula, bala!" Englehorn told the chief reassuringly. "Tomorrow, friend."

The retreat gathered speed; but not too much speed. There was no lagging, but on the other hand there was no undue haste. Only an expeditious, smiling withdrawal. A half dozen sailors led by Driscoll went first, with Ann in their center. Next the main body moved, rifles alert. Englehorn followed these and Denham went last.

As a parting sign of friendship his hand tossed the witch doctor a debonair salute. The same hand cocked his hat over one eye, and as the hand dropped, to a holstered pistol, his lips puckered up to whistle a marching tune. While the natives' eyes widened in surprise he slid briskly around the corner of the house and out of the tribe's sight.

Following the narrow paths, among houses as silent and seemingly as uninhabited as had been encountered on the inward trek, the Wanderer's party came at length to the edge of the village. Forward extended the almost treeless stretch of land running down to the beach and the boats.

"Don't tell me there wasn't nobody in them houses," Jimmy snorted, shifting his box of bombs to the other shoulder. "I heard a kid squall once. And boy! What a smack his mama handed him. I heard that, too."

Driscoll, with a half laugh of relief, let go the small hand he had held protectingly all along the march.

"Believe it or not," he said with a last backward glance, "nobody is following us. And if that isn't a surprise as unexpected as it is pleasant, I want to know."

Denham and Englehorn came trotting up.

"I hope," Ann laughed, half at them, and half at Driscoll, "that you all know me well enough to understand I'm no warlike, bragging Brunhilde. But just the same, I want to say I wouldn't have missed it for the mint."

She nodded emphatically, and with a broad pretense of pride began to fluff out the hair which had been so much admired.

Driscoll eyed her provoking mouth with an exasperation which did not conceal his admiration for her courage.

"You can be my next leading lady, too," Denham promised.

Englehorn cut himself a fresh chew and waved them all to the boats.

"Tomorrow," he said, "we'll break out the trade goods. I think, Mr. Denham, a few presents to that witch doctor ought to get us somewhere."

Chapter 8

When they were gathered in the skipper's cabin back on the Wanderer, Denham put the question which had grown steadily in all minds during the long row out from the beach. He spoke somberly, to a somber audience. In the moment of arrival at the boats, their mood had been one of exhilaration over the lucky outcome of their encounter. Now, however, they had had time to ponder the danger they had run . . . and even more than that, the ominous mystery which prompted Denham to speak.

"I want to know," he said, "who this Kong is, that the king and the witch doctor jabbered about."

"Mightn't he be the king himself?" asked Ann.

"No," Englehorn declared. "You saw how frightened that young girl was. She wouldn't have been frightened, not much anyway, if they'd fixed her up for the boss. She'd have been happy, more likely. Going to him would have been big luck. But she was scared half out of her senses."

"I think those islanders dressed up as gorillas are the key," Driscoll said.

"Why?" Denham wanted to know, and eyed his assistant speculatively.

"Just a hunch. I figure they were acting as the real bridegroom's representatives. On top of that big gate, there hung a huge metal drum. And beside it I saw a native ready to sound off. And I'm ready to swear that when the king saw us and stopped the show, he was about to direct the opening of the gate."

"I think I follow you," Denham said.

"Well, I don't!" Ann exclaimed. "I'm completely in the dark."

"The king," Driscoll explained slowly, "was about to send the girl out to whatever is beyond the gate. Now what could that be? The whole village is on this side, safely behind the wall. Beyond, there could be nothing but wild jungle—and that danger against which the tribe maintains the wall.

"The king was going to open the gate in order to offer the girl to whatever feared thing lives in the jungle. He was sending out a bride to Kong. And the fellow up at the drum was going to call Kong to come and get her."

Denham nodded.

"My guess," Englehorn murmured, "is that today's pretty little girl wasn't by any means the first of Kong's brides."

"You mean . . ." Ann felt suddenly sick.

"He means," Driscoll broke in roughly, "that the girl was a sacrifice. And that there is a fresh sacrifice at regular intervals . . . every time the moon is full, or something like that."

"But even agreeing to all this," Englehorn puzzled, "I haven't yet any clear idea of what Kong is."

"I have," Denham said with abrupt conviction. "That wall wasn't built against any pint-sized danger. There were a dozen proxy bridegrooms because only with so many could the natives approximate the size of the creature which was getting the sacrifice. And those gorilla skins that the dancers wore didn't mean that Kong is a gorilla by a long shot. If he's really there, he's a brute big enough to use a gorilla for a medicine ball."

"But there never was such a beast!" Ann laughed uncertainly. "At least not since prehistoric times."

Denham shifted in his seat to stare.

"Holy Mackerel!" he whispered. "I wonder if you've hit it, Ann?"

"Rot!" Driscoll exploded.

Englehorn shook an unbelieving head.

"Don't be so sure," Denham argued, and excitement mounted in him again, as it had at the first sight of land. "Remember? Both of you said we wouldn't find any Skull Mountain Island. But here it is.

"Why shouldn't such an out-of-the-way spot be just the place to find a solitary, surviving prehistoric freak?" His eyes flashed. "Holy Mackerel! If we did find the brute, what a picture!"

The shock of that expressed hope sent Driscoll to his feet.

"Where will Ann figure in a picture like that?" he demanded.

Denham rose, too, in angry response to the challenging question. But, after an instant, he laughed.

"Jack," he said plaintively, "can't you let me run my own show? I suppose you had to go soft. And I guess Ann is plenty excuse. But don't expect me to pass up the picture there'll be if we really *get* the break I'm imagining."

He pulled thoughtfully at one ear.

"I'll admit," he conceded, "that right now I can't think just where any of us will figure. That'll need a lot of doping out."

"Um-m-m-m!" Englehorn agreed.

"Here's what!" Denham went on. "We'll sign off everything until after supper. By then I'll have at least the next step planned."

"In the meantime," Englehorn said, "you see to posting a few guards with rifles, Mr. Driscoll. That old witch doctor is up to something. The drums have started up again."

While the four talked the drums had indeed gradually renewed their rolling. Their cadence was different now: a low drone, as of men thinking aloud, or better yet of the sound primitive hands might beat out in order to make easier for primitive minds the hard business of thinking.

With the guards posted, Driscoll came back to Englehorn, and looked toward the sky.

"There'll be plenty of clouds to hide the moon," he predicted. "It'll be a dark night. And that isn't going to help."

"Mr. Denham is right," the skipper joked him placidly. "You've gone soft over Ann. A dark night won't hurt. We're too far off shore for the natives to try a surprise."

"I don't like those drums!"

The drums continued to trouble Driscoll as the quick, tropic twilight fell and deepened, but when he sat down to supper he tried to conceal his anxiety. This was harder because Denham kept them all waiting for his promised plan.

"I told you I'd figure out the next step," he

finally began at the close of the meal, "and I have. I've got no farther; but at least I've made up my mind to this. I'm going ashore bright and early tomorrow. With a strong party there'll be no danger. And I've absolutely got to find out about Kong."

Driscoll pushed his coffee cup away and looked toward Ann.

"Drink hearty, Jack," Denham smiled. "Ann will stay snug and safe on board ship."

"Good," murmured Englehorn.

"I'm ready to go if you need me," Ann spoke up.

"No. Ordinarily, I'm dead against separating my cast from my camera. But ordinarily my people have to face only dangers I can measure and prepare against. Here we have an unknown quantity. So I'll leave you in safety while I go for a look-see."

"Let me look for you," Driscoll said eagerly. "Of course there won't be any danger, with a strong party. But if you should happen to get hurt, the picture would be held up. If I bump into a tree, or something, it won't matter."

"Oh, won't it?" Ann cried.

"Ready to die for dear old Rutgers, Driscoll, now I've let Ann off?" Denham chuckled. "Well, you can go straight to hell, son. When I organize a parade, I always lead it.

"But just the same," he went on, "I take back part of what I said about you going soft.

I guess you're soft in only one spot."

Driscoll flushed down to his neck and back to his closely set ears.

"I've got some work to polish off below," he said and retreated before Englehorn's and Denham's laughter.

"I," said Ann with great dignity, getting up, too, "am not amused." But she smiled back at them as she went out to the deck.

The drums were still droning thoughtfully on Skull Mountain Island. On the deck, at intervals, the armed guards made watchful silhouettes. A few other sailors were out, too, seeking relief from the heat which had succeeded the fog. Lumpy was one of these. Stretched out on a hatch, in his frayed trousers, he played lazily with Ignatz.

"Good evening, Lumpy."

"Evenin', Miss Ann. Move over, Ignatz; give the lady a seat. I hear you had a big time ashore."

"I was pretty scared."

They sat for a little, Lumpy too lethargic to talk, Ann soothed by the soft blackness.

Denham and Englehorn halted on their way to the bridge.

"Hear those drums!" Denham said. "Damn it, if I could take moving pictures by firelight, I'd sneak back there this minute."

"You're a lot better off here, Mr. Denham."

"*I* know! But I hate to miss anything."

"It's all right with me if we miss a lot."

"Look here, Skipper! It's enough to have Driscoll worrying."

"I'm hardly worrying. But I'm glad a guard is set. And I have half a notion not to turn in."

"Pshaw! All the natives are busy ashore."

"I suppose so. But still, I think I'll stay around."

"I'll stay, too, then," Denham laughed. "We'll start a good game of pinochle."

Lumpy sat up and peered at Ann through the darkness.

"What ever happened ashore to get that cold old turtle so het up?" he demanded.

"I think," said Ann slowly, "that it must have been the girl."

"Girl?"

"The one they were sacrificing . . . to Kong."

"Oh, yeah!" Lumpy nodded. "Some of the boys were telling me. The bride."

"The bride of Kong!" Ann whispered, and shivered. "Lumpy, what do you suppose Kong is?"

"Ah-h-h!" Lumpy declared scornfully. "Just an old heathen god. Every tribe has a god. Usually an old log or mud statue. I'll bet Kong's just a lump of mud, and that the bride never gets within a mile of him. The old witch doctor probably could tell you better where *she* goes. Them old witch doctors usually have a harem hid off somewheres."

Ann laughed, and shifting a little for a more comfortable position sat on Ignatz's leg. That sensitive monkey squeaked and fled indignantly.

"Catch him, Lumpy," Ann said. "He'll get into the cabins and break something."

"Here, you varmint!" Lumpy called and ran.

Ann rose, and lifted her arms sleepily. She was rested and relaxed by the talk with Lumpy; she could forget Kong now. She walked slowly down to where the deck became a narrow alley leading past the deckhouse.

For just an instant she hesitated there. The light from the deckhouse glinted on her yellow hair, before she moved on, into the thick swallowing darkness. The drums on Skull Mountain Island swelled to a deafening clamor, then fell to a low chuckling tattoo.

Up on the bridge Denham talked confidently to Englehorn.

"We'll make friends with 'em, all right, Skipper. They didn't like our breaking into the ceremony. But we can convince them that was an accident."

"I don't know," Englehorn demurred. "They said we spoiled the show. They probably meant they'd have to find Kong another bride."

"Great! If they do it all over again, I'll get a picture as sure as shooting."

Englehorn looked at his employer in incredulous admiration.

"You're the limit," he declared, and felt around with a foot for the cuspidor he knew was somewhere in the darkness.

Driscoll came up, wiping his forehead.

"I've just made the rounds," he said, "and everything looks as right as rain. Where's Ann?"

"On deck somewhere, I suppose. How long is it since you saw her?" Denham chuckled. "A whole half hour?"

"I'm glad," Driscoll drawled, "that *I'm* no cold-blooded fish," and he strolled down to the main deck.

Lumpy was there, looking at the hatch with an air of puzzlement.

"Seen Miss Darrow, Lumpy?"

"She was here ten minutes ago, sir. We wuz talkin' and the monk got loose, and she sent me off to catch him. I thought she'd still be here when I got back."

"Probably she went in to her cabin," Driscoll surmised.

Lumpy, leading Ignatz, started away in disappointment. His path led down the narrow alley into which Ann had disappeared, and as he stepped into it, his foot struck something. He stooped, picked it up, brought it back to the lighter area by the hatch.

"On deck!" he shouted the next instant. "On deck! All hands on deck!"

The guards took up the cry, and sailors appeared from everywhere. Driscoll, running back, came up against Englehorn and Denham as they raced down from the bridge. All three closed in on Lumpy.

"Look, sir!" the old sailor stammered. "I found this on deck!"

"A native bracelet!" cried Denham.

"Some of them heathens've been aboard, sir!"

"Search the ship, Skipper," Denham ordered.

"Where's Ann?" Driscoll cried.

Englehorn and Denham looked at one another; then the skipper flashed off to direct the search.

"In her cabin . . ." Denham began soothingly.

"She isn't! I've just looked!"

The voice of a guard on the island side of the Wanderer floated to the two men: "No, sir! I never heard a sound. Not a thing." Then Englehorn's crisp, commanding tones. "Bos'n. Man the boats. A rifle to every man."

The darkness became alive with sounds. The bos'n's whistle. The creak and thump of davits.

The rattle of arms. The low, directing cries of the sailors at work.

Denham stared at Driscoll.

"The boats!" he said explosively. "The boats! Here, Skipper! You don't really think . . ."

"I don't know," Englehorn replied. "But we won't lose any time finding out. Mr. Driscoll, you take charge of the party searching the ship. And work fast, my boy! Work fast!"

Chapter 9

Hot, native hands thrust Ann down to the bottom of the silently racing dugout. One was pressed over her mouth, and though she twisted wildly she could send no cry back through the darkness to the Wanderer.

No single cry had been permitted her from the first instant of capture. Hot, pressing hands had bound and gagged her always. Her mouth had felt them first, as she stepped into the narrow, black aisle beside the deckhouse; and mouth, arms and legs had been clamped as she was passed from hands to other hands down the ship's side.

Ann was afraid in a way that she had never imagined. No book she had ever read, no story

she had ever been told could equal the terror
which swept her in increasing waves. It was a
terror which made her feel that every inch of
her insulted body was alive with unmention-
able things. It went beyond the midnight horrors of childhood. It went beyond the horrors
of dreams. Her single conscious thought was to
cry out for help, but she told herself despair-
ingly that even if the hand lifted from her
mouth it would do no good. Her throat, she
knew, would refuse to give forth utterance.

Her legs, released at last, did indeed refuse
to act. When the dugout grated ashore and
her captors jerked her to her feet on the beach,
she could not stand.

Wasting no time, two bulking shadows swung her to their shoulders and raced
off through the darkness toward the village.
Several times in the course of the flight the
bearers were changed. This always followed a
high-pitched command. And the third time she
heard it Ann's heart leaped to a realization that
the speaker was the witch doctor.

The ceremonial court before the wall's great
gate was bright with torches. The tribe was
massed here, just as it had been massed in the
afternoon. The same ordered rows lined either
side of the skin-covered bridal dais. The same
black gorilla men occupied the two front
ranks. The king had taken his same aloof
stand, clad in the same magnificence of

feathers, grass and fur. And the witch doctor, leaving Ann's bearers to stand guard where she had been put down, promptly took his own proper position.

The dais, halfway up the broad stone stairs, was empty. Ann's fear-numbed mind, however, failed to see the significance of that. Close by her, a pitying face stood out from the crowd, and Ann vaguely recognized the flower-garlanded girl of the afternoon, dressed now as all the other women were dressed. That meant nothing, either. And when, at the witch doctor's signal, she was picked up and borne to the dais she sat there in an uncomprehending stupor.

Nervous haste had pulsed behind the command which put Ann into her place. The witch doctor had belabored his paddlers all the way back from the Wanderer. He had forced Ann's bearers to their highest speed on the race to the village. Now he was even more swift to set the ceremony going. Ann realized dimly that so much haste was due to a conviction that rescuers would be quick in pursuit. But the realization aroused no hope. She had been totally without hope from the moment her first cry had been stifled. She had had her own inescapable conviction that the mystery of this ancient island had trapped her and that no rescue was possible.

At a signal, the massed natives began a familiar chant. Their serried ranks swayed in the torchlight in an hypnotic rhythm. The witch doctor advanced to the dais and once more performed his oddly supplicating dance. Once more the gorilla men leaped out from the chanting host.

And now, as in the afternoon, another signal brought the king into the ceremony. He stepped forward, and at his commanding arm ten warriors rushed at the two smoothly trimmed half logs which held the great gate shut.

"Ndeze!"

Ann needed no knowledge of the language to know the king had shouted, "Open!" Five men to each bar, the gate-tenders strained and slowly drew the wooden bolts back through massive, time-pitted iron sockets. With still greater straining each group began to pull its half of the great gate open.

"Ndundo!" the king shouted.

Instantly a warrior who had been standing on the gate's high portal struck a mighty blow against the metal drum suspended above. Briefly aroused by the rolling sound, Ann realized that the signal forecast by Driscoll had been given.

It was a signal to others besides whatever bridegroom waited in the wilderness outside the wall. At the blow upon the drum the chanting ceased. The massed ranks on either

side of the dais broke. With cries of mingled
excitement and apprehension the tribesmen,
and the women and children as well, fled to
the wall. By frail ladders, they scrambled to
the top.

Once on the lofty rampart the tribe resumed
its chant, to the accompaniment of swaying
torches held so as to cast most of their smoky
light beyond the wall.

"Tasko!" the king shouted.

Now the guards picked Ann up, dais and
all, and rushed her through the opening gate.

"Watu!" the king shouted.

Instantly the gate-tenders all but joined the
doors of the gate. Only the narrowest gap was
left, and then ten men braced themselves to
close even this on the instant of the return of
the dais bearers. Indeed, from their grim ex-
pressions, it was plain they meant to close the
gap, if necessary, before the bearers got back.

"Ndundo!" the king shouted, and once
again the drummer rolled thunder out to the
black wilderness.

High on the walls the tribespeople tipped
their torches for a better view.

Beyond the wall a brief plain ran off and
lost itself in the darkly shadowed base of the
precipice. In this plain, a few rods out, stood
a stone altar as ancient as the wall it faced. Its
steeply ascending steps were spotted with
hoary lichens. Its platform, some dozen feet

above the ground, lay under inches of furry green moss which soaked up the torches' light. Two worn pillars, splendidly carved, rose out of the platform a short arm's width apart.

"Tasko! Tasko!" the king shouted.

As his voice leaped through the crack of the gate Ann's bearers raced her at a redoubled speed up the slippery steps of the altar and swung her into position between the pillars. Two spread her arms while two more tied grass ropes to her wrists, cast loops around the pillars and drew them tight. Ann hung, barely conscious, her eyes closed.

"Ndundo!" the king shouted, this time to the drummer on the wall.

The man swung his blunt stick again. The thunder rolled deafeningly. The crowded rampart swayed in an insane chant. Ann's bearers leaped to the ground and, with fearful glances backward, fled. The gate closed upon the heels of the last one, and Ann was alone, without the wall.

From the shadowed base of the precipice came a deep, unreal roar which met the roll of the drum and threw it back against the wall.

"Kong!" The watching, torch-illumined mob on the rampart burst into a great cry. "Kong! Kong! Kong!"

A sense of impending fate lifted Ann's eyelids. She stared about in bewilderment, uncertain where she was. She looked at her wrists, and realizing now what hurt her she struggled erect to lessen the ropes' bite.

Before her, she became conscious of the crowded wall. Behind her she was aware of a closer, deeper shout, and of a Shadow. She turned her head. Then, while her eyes widened, the Shadow split the black cloak of the precipice and became solidly real. Blinking up at the packed wall, its vast mouth roared defiance, its black, furred hands drummed a black, furred breast in challenge. In the full glare of the torches it hesitated, stopped and as though reading the meaning of the thousand hands which gestured from the rampart, turned and looked down at the altar, and at Ann.

It did not look *up* at Ann upon her pedestal. It looked *down*. Moving closer it stared down between the two pillars. High up on the wall the tribespeople caught their breath. Their pointing arms grew motionless. Even the torch flames seemed to cease their wavering. And Ann's scream sped piercingly into a dead silence.

Kong jerked back a half step and rumbled angrily. His great hand, which had been about to touch the curious, golden crest revealed by the torches, withdrew. He turned and stared suspiciously up at the wall, but when no further sound came from the crowded natives

there, and no sound or further movement from
the figure now drooping between the pillars,
he renewed his investigation.

Immediately he found that he could not
pick Ann up, and shortly he found the reason.
The ropes, however, offered no difficulty. The
loops about the pillars broke in his hands and
he was free to explore the amazing being who
drooped across his arm. Shining hair, petalled
cheek, tissue garments, puzzling footgear . . .
his fingers discovered endless mystery. In an
intensity of preoccupation he began to rumble
to himself as he turned the figure over, this
way and that, much in the manner that a half-
adult human being might turn and inspect a
limp unconscious bird.

When the crowd shouted again, he did not
even look up. When new voices joined the
clamor he paid no more attention. With a last,
intent look at the white countenance beneath
his hand, he shifted Ann's form to the crook
of one arm and started slowly back into the
shadow of the precipice. The heavy creak of
the opening gate drew no sign from his re-
ceding back. And when a challenging figure
plunged through, and cried loudly, and shot a
whistling something past his ear, he only
leaped more quickly over the last few yards
which separated him from the black concealing wilderness.

Chapter 10

It had been Denham who raced the rescue boats away from the Wanderer; and Denham who had deployed the sailors for the breathless run to the village. But from the moment the great gate swung open Driscoll took charge. It was Driscoll who organized the pursuit after Kong.

He alone had got a fair look at the beast god lumbering into the darkness with Ann's bright head cradled in one arm. The shot which accelerated Kong's last step had been his.

"This is my job," he had said to Denham, and the director nodded, "O.K. Jack. We'll do it together."

"I'll need a dozen of you," Driscoll cried,

turning back to the crew. "Who's coming with me?"

"I'll go," Lumpy volunteered, and back of him the others called out with raised hands.

"You keep watch here, Lumpy," Driscoll said. "I'll take you!" he pointed. "And you! And you! . . ."

"Who's got the bombs?" Denham asked. "We'll need them."

"Here they are," Jimmy cried, and when a bigger man offered to take them, he drew back jealously. "Not much, guy! I lugged them before. I can lug 'em now."

"We'll leave the Skipper in charge here. Right?" Driscoll said to Denham.

The director nodded. Together, the two inspected guns, ammunition and flashlights.

"Single file," Driscoll ordered. "Never lose sight of the man ahead of you. And follow me."

He set off at a trot, Denham beside him. At the altar he paused and measured the height of the pillars with his eyes. When he had done, he looked at Denham incredulously.

"You got a glimpse of it too, didn't you?" Denham nodded.

"I can't believe it," Driscoll said. "I got a fair look. I saw that Thing's head squarely in line with the top of those pillars and they stand twenty feet above the ground if they stand an inch." He shivered. "Come on," he ended. "This is wasting time."

On the left, as they came to the base of the precipice, they heard water flowing in the darkness. Denham suggested that this might be a guide to some crevice which would lead them up to the plateau; so they stumbled toward it.

They found a stream. In one direction the water flowed off toward the wall. In the other, the bed of the stream ran steeply up through a narrow split in the precipice. The natural crevice inclined just steeply enough to send the water down in a swift deep slide, but no more.

"As good a swimmer as you are, Jack," said Denham, "could come down that chute."

Driscoll nodded and went about the difficult business of finding a trail up. He had just found what looked like a possible path along the water's edge when one of the party called out.

"Here's a track!"

Driscoll turned his flashlights upon the mark of a foot so large that the men stared in unbelief; but it pointed up along the very trail Driscoll had picked out.

"Let's go," he said.

In the darkness it was cruel going. A cracked shin, a bruising stumble marked nearly every yard of the way. Once a man slipped into the swift water and shot down a hundred feet before he found a ledge to cling to.

"I kept my gun," he gasped cheerfully, as he was pulled out.

Up on top of the precipice they encountered jungle at the very outset. Enormous trees, and at their bases a lush tangle of undergrowth. The stream, widening somewhat, extended back into the country which seemed to rise higher and higher.

"We'll find that this plateau slopes gradually back to Skull Mountain," Denham surmised.

Nowhere was there any sign of a trail, and for a moment all were nonplussed.

"Look for a track again," Driscoll ordered.

"Here is broken down brush," a sailor said. "Something big has gone through."

The breaks were fresh, too.

"And here's that track again," cried another.

The track was in a clear space beyond the broken brush, and once more it pointed upstream. It was clue enough, and Driscoll led the way as fast as he could in the darkness.

"There's a bird call," Denham said after a little. "Hear it? A lot of them."

The silence did, indeed, suddenly pulse with bird cries and the reviving whirr and flick of insects.

"It's dawn," Denham exulted. "Now we'll get a break, Jack."

"Now we'll put on speed," Driscoll promised.

For a space, no change was apparent. They

still moved through what seemed an utter blackness. Then, slowly, they could catch shadows at a distance. Next, whenever they paused to puzzle out the way, they marched ahead upon a trail grown a little plainer. And finally, unmistakably, light began to filter down.

It was a shaft of this which gave them their next encouragement. It pointed to another of the great footprints.

"Look at the size of the thing!" Jimmy exploded, shifting his bombs. "He must be as big as a house."

"He came this way, all right," Denham said to Driscoll.

"And he was headed the way we're going. Come on."

"Keep those guns ready," Denham reminded the men.

"*He's* telling *us*," grunted Jimmy.

A wide glade opened to their weary feet. Bruised by the trees they had not been able to avoid in the darkness, stung by branches which had whipped them at every step, they stumbled into it thankfully. It was now full daylight. Except for a thin drifting mist every tree, every bush, every strand of knee deep grass was clearly visible.

Once again they came upon a footprint and once again it led on in the direction they had been going.

Driscoll had started off at a trot when Denham called out in alarm. Halting, Driscoll looked to a flank along the line of the director's extended arm. Behind him the sailors burst into panic-stricken cries.

"Kong!" someone cried. But it was not Kong.

An immense beast was emerging from the jungle, a beast with thick, scaly hide, a huge spiked tail, and a small reptilian head upon a long swaying neck. It walked in an awkward squatting posture upon tremendous hind legs. Its forelegs were carried elevated far up toward the base of the long neck and were more like paws.

The sailors stared in confused unbelief, but Denham and Driscoll grew cold from their first full realization of the true scope of the island's mystery.

"Jimmy," Denham cried. "Where are the bombs?"

He seized one as the beast turned in their direction.

"When I throw," he called loudly, "everybody must drop in his tracks, and keep his face pressed close to the earth."

Still at the edge of the jungle, the beast widened its nostrils and drew in the puzzling scent of the strange creatures in the glade. Full of this, it started upon a clumsy, open-mouthed attack.

The sailors scattered, Jimmy a slow last because of his burden now become doubly precious. Only Denham and Driscoll stood fast. The latter pumped two rifle shots into the swaying head with no effect. Denham waited patiently for the target to come closer.

"When you drop," he said unhurriedly, "keep close to me and don't get up until I do."

Then he threw.

The missile struck squarely in front of the beast's feet. Its instant explosion enveloped feet, scaly body and small head in a thick blue vapor.

"Down!" Denham shouted, and flung himself to the ground.

As Driscoll dropped alongside, the director put a hand on his mate's face to make sure it pressed close to the ground.

Driscoll breathed in the damp rich smell of earth, and the sap of growing roots grew bitter upon his lips. Just forward the ground shook from the fall of a great weight. He would have got up, but Denham's hand pressed warningly. Finally the hand lifted and then tapped his shoulder.

Driscoll stood up. Scarcely the length of his own body away lay the outstretched, twitching head of the beast. Back of the head the body rose like an enormous mound. The mate was amazed at the beast's proximity.

"Good Lord!" he exclaimed. "It came a good fifty feet after it got the gas."

"But I stopped it," Denham said triumph-antly. "Didn't I tell you one of those bombs would stop anything?"

"Is it dead?"

"No," Denham said. "But that's just a de-tail." He picked up his gun, walked forward, felt for the beast's heart and shot twice. The great body started convulsively and then grew rigid. Denham hesitated, then for good meas-ure sent a bullet through the reptilian head.

Backing off to Driscoll, he stared with some-thing of the unbelief of the sailors who now came slowly back.

"Prehistoric life!" he ejaculated and turning to Driscoll he cried out: "Jack! She was right last night on the ship. Ann, I mean. But she only had the start of it. She guessed the beast-god was some primitive survival. But if this thing we've killed means anything, the plateau is alive with all sorts of creatures that have survived along with Kong."

Driscoll looked to see no dirt had fouled his rifle, and beckoned the sailors.

"Look for tracks!" he ordered.

"My own guess," he said slowly, as the men scattered, "is that you'll find plenty of sur-vivals. And that you won't like them half as much as you think."

Tracks were easy to find in the light of day. A half dozen men reported them, and in a little while the trail was resumed. It still led along the stream, but the land now sloped downward.

"The mist is thickening," Jimmy complained.

"Thickening!" Denham said. "Look there!"

A hollow lay ahead of them. The stream ran into it, and where the hollow sank deepest the morning mist had become almost a cloud of fog. In the midst of this, they heard a splashing.

"Think it's him?" Denham said.

"We'll find out," Driscoll cried, and raced ahead.

He was waiting in exasperation at the water's edge when the others caught up with him. Beside him was a fresh footprint not yet filled with water although that speeded quickly into any depression made on the bank.

"He got across," he said, and waved to the stream which widened almost to a small lake in the hollow. "We've got to swim."

"That's out." Denham shook his head. "We can't swim with guns and bombs."

"Then we can do better," Driscoll said and pointed to two logs resting against the shore. "We'll build a raft."

"Good!" Denham agreed.

"All right, boys," Driscoll called. "We're going to ferry over. On a raft."

The sailors nodded, but before they could

spread out to hunt for more logs and for stout, pliable vines to use as ropes, Driscoll beckoned them soberly.

"Here's something you ought to know," he said and briefly told of the conclusion he and Denham had drawn after studying the beast just slain. "This may be more than you bargained for," he ended. "If anyone of you wants to go back, now's the time to shove off."

The men looked at one another. Finally Jimmy put a question.

"You say that maybe we'll want to back out because we've never seen any of these big lobsters? Is that the idea?"

Driscoll nodded.

"Well!" Jimmy said with a pleased glance at his bombs, "they haven't seen us either. That makes it fifty-fifty. I guess we'll stick."

Chapter 11

Everybody worked at top speed, Driscoll fastest of all. He dared not risk the moment's idleness which would enable the suppressed picture of Ann as he had last seen her to push too far forward into his mind. He had another reason, too. Denham was plainly waiting for an opportunity to say how he blamed himself, how sorry he was. Driscoll felt he couldn't bear that, either.

The raft was finished quickly. There were vines in abundance, and the half score of logs they required were easily found; this lagoon-like widening of the stream seemed a catch-all for everything that fell into its waters farther up.

"How deep do you think it is?" Driscoll wondered.

"Not over ten or fifteen feet most of the distance," Denham guessed. "But from the way the grass disappears in the center, and the stillness of the water there, I think we may hit a pot-hole going down to the mines."

"We can paddle a little then."

Veiled in the still perceptible mist, the sailors clambered carefully aboard, each with a pole in addition to his rifle. There was scarcely room for the last man. He managed to get on only by the narrowest fit.

"Don't get the guns wet," Denham warned.

"Oke!" said Jimmy for them all.

"All set?" Driscoll looked around.

"Setting pretty!"

"Watch those bombs, Jimmy!"

"Ain't I watching?"

"All right! Shove off."

They were away with a jerk and a clumsy roll that all but toppled the hindside men into the water. These were saved by their poles and presently were shoving with cautious earnestness along with the others.

Everyone was suddenly dead sober. The fog; a reaction from the forced bits of jocularity at the start; the thought of Ann, which was almost as heavy a weight upon the minds of the sailors as upon Driscoll's, all helped to darken their mood. The raft was no very tractable craft, either, and the problem it offered helped to lower their spirits.

"Easy now," Denham said. " 'Ware the balance. Don't let her swing."

One edge of the raft went awash.

"Keep your weight toward center," Driscoll cautioned. "Well toward center."

They were in the middle now, and as Denham had predicted the poles found no bottom; not even a hint of one. It was necessary to use them as paddles, and this added to the danger of capsizing. The poles were badly balanced, and any sweeping movement that had real force behind it tipped the raft ominously.

"I think I see weeds ahead," Driscoll said. "We'll find bottom there. What's that?"

The stern of the raft had scraped over something. A knob? The upward jutting end of a water-soaked log?

"Christ!" Jimmy burst forth.

A strangled ranging bellow followed close upon the blow, and then, a little astern, reared a great scaly head and a section of a great scaly body.

"Dinosaur!" Denham exploded. "By the Power! A dinosaur!"

His tone was a mingling of consternation and the triumphant excitement of discovery.

The monstrous apparition threw the men into a panic. Paddles swung wildly. Only their unlooked for arrival in shallower water, where the poles served as props, saved the raft. Even at that it tilted precariously and one man was pushed off. By luck his hand closed on a trailing length of vine-rope and he dragged along behind, slowing the flight.

The huge head curved to the water and dived. A broad scaly back rose to the surface; then it, too, vanished.

"Push!" Driscoll ordered swiftly. "It's trying to come up under us. We're nearly there. Everybody, now! Heave-ho!"

The last pound of power went into a few final, desperate thrusts. Ten times the power, however, would not have made their speed equal to that of the great shadow which moved swiftly beneath them. They were still a fair stone's throw from shore when the raft took a tremendous blow from underneath.

"The bombs!" Denham shouted. "Save 'em, Jimmy!"

Jimmy was barely able to save himself; and Denham's tardy snatch for one of the missiles missed, although he had dropped his rifle in the effort to secure it. Everyone was thrown violently into the water. The raft itself was torn into its ten original parts. One of these toppled on the head of the man who had been towing astern. He went under heavily and did not reappear.

The others struggled toward shore like scattering sheep.

Well in the lead, Driscoll threshed forward at a racing pace. Already he had headed to where he might again pick up the trail of the beast god. Denham, a good waterman himself, was next. A little to the left went Jimmy, minus his iron burden at last.

The half-emerging dinosaur still lurched among the fragments of the raft. The tremendous blow it had struck, the veiling mist and the shower of logs had brought a short confusion. Except for that, few of the men would have got away. As it was, all save one were scrambling over the far bank when the beast's head cleared. That one, the beast sighted and to him it gave chase in a series of lunging, elephantine strides.

Driscoll paused at the water's edge long enough to give a hand to Denham and Jimmy and one or two more, and with these as a nucleus swung left on a dead run calling to the others to follow. As they ran, the ground ascended and the mist disappeared.

Driscoll came finally to a high narrow crest beyond which the ground sloped again down to a wide morass. It was a soft, blackish expanse with here and there areas where the surface had hardened under the sun and cracked into great slabs. Denham, joining him, stared at this and interpreted again as he had interpreted the appearance of the dinosaur.

"Asphalt!" he said. "An asphalt morass that

was there before the first beast came into being. A sink of hell! There'll be thousands of
carcasses buried rods deep in it. If we try to
cross, Jack, we'll have to be careful we don't
stick and sink, too."

Driscoll nodded and turning around shouted
a loud summons.

A curious phenomenon lay in the direction
of the stream. Close by, clear sunlight flashed
upon the brush and the wet faces of men who
came breathless up the rendezvous. Farther
back the steeply descending ground was covered by the mist which hung motionlessly
there in a deep layer thick enough to cast a
veil over everything. Through it, as through
thin white smoke, more of the party struggled
up toward the crest. Driscoll began counting
these distant survivors and then the others
closer at hand.

"Look!" Denham cried.

Following his pointing hand to the far side
of the valley out of which they had climbed,
they saw a single figure, dwarfed by distance
to less than quarter size, racing violently toward the trees. It was the last man. He had
taken the wrong direction, and behind him
lumbered a giant, huge headed pursuer.

"Stand fast!" Denham cautioned as Driscoll stepped impulsively forward. No one, he
pointed out, could get there in time, and the

others, gathering around, made that plain by their rigid immobility.

The midget managed to get to a tree, and by a miracle of despairing strength climbed into its lower branches. The dinosaur paused beneath and reached its vast mouth up with a seemingly slow care.

"Hasn't anybody got a gun?" Denham asked furiously.

"They're all at the bottom of the stream," Driscoll muttered.

"If we only had one of them bombs," a sailor cried, "we could run back and maybe do something yet."

"I had to let them go to keep from drowning," Jimmy stammered.

"That was a lunkheaded trick," Denham told him. "You could have saved a couple."

"*You* lost your *gun.*"

"Come to think of it," Denham admitted with a wry grin, "I did."

Except for the sheath knives which Driscoll and several of the sailors carried, no weapons remained.

They all stared again across the valley. Through the mist the dinosaur's grotesque head reached up, until only a threadlike strand of light separated it from the man's body in the tree. A thin, distant scream drifted to their ears. Head and body merged. The little

group upon the crest drew closer to one another. One of the sailors turned suddenly and
violently sick. Another would have burst in
fury down the slope toward his comrade but
Denham tripped him up.

"We'll go along," Driscoll said, and turned
back to consider the problem of the asphalt
morass. "Scatter out, you men, and see if you
can pick up a footprint."

He, himself, felt sick from wondering how
many of the crew were to go before they
caught up with Kong, and how many after-
wards. Thinking of the beast-god, his mind
called up the picture he had seen in the frame
of the altar's pillars. The picture was so vivid
that at first, as he gazed across the morass, he
thought that what he saw was simply imagination. The shouts of the rest told him otherwise; the picture was real.

The beast-god they sought was lumbering
toward them from the center of the asphalt
field. Monstrous beyond conception, as hairy
as any of the simian creatures of an African
jungle whom he resembled in all but size, the
fact that he picked his way with a slow, almost
human caution, made him all the more incredible.

Incredible, too, was the care with which he
bore Ann. His primitive brain valued this
strange possession for reasons it could not understand. Much as a prehistoric woman might

have cradled her baby, he carried the girl's inert form in the crook of one arm. Almost, the watchers would have sworn, there was purpose in the way his broad back was interposed between his captive and the vast pursuing beasts which plodded inexorably behind, doggedly wresting their great feet from the suck of the asphalt.

These obviously were still more of the gigantic creatures which had survived on Skull Mountain Island from a forgotten age. Huge, four-legged things they were, with thick short necks and short heavy heads ending in horns. There were three horns on each head, short, pointed weapons which shook implacably after Kong.

Both Kong and his pursuers were so intent upon one another that the watchers on the crest had gone unnoticed.

"Down!" Driscoll commanded. "Down!"

All flung themselves behind the concealing mask of some bushes.

"If we only had our bombs!" Denham groaned.

"What are those brutes?" Driscoll asked.

"Tri—" Denham hesitated over the word he knew well enough but had spoken probably never, having always been content to leave it in the book in which he found it. "Wait a moment. I have it. Triceratopses."

"And what are they?"

"Just another of Nature's mistakes, Jack. Something like a dinosaur. But with their fore-legs more fully developed. They got their names from the three horns on their heads."

The pursuit had drawn closer to Kong. He stood now on a dry mound in the center of the morass. He had put Ann down on the far side of the mound, away from the triceratopses. The farthest behind of these was apparently out of the fight, and out of all other fights as well. It had lumbered into a spot too soft to walk upon and was speeding its own end by fruitless struggles. The other two, however, were al-most at the edge of the mound. Luckier than their companion, they had picked out dry paths and were sure to reach their objective.

Already Kong was carrying on a long dis-tance fire. Great slabs of the hardened asphalt swung up over his snarling face and went hurtling down upon the triceratopses' horny heads.

"No!" Denham said as he watched. "I won't believe it. There never was a beast as strong as that."

What amazed him, and all the others, was the power with which Kong cast his huge pro-jectiles. One, striking fairly, broke off a horn. The triceratops staggered, obviously hurt, and Kong redoubled his attack. The second of the two beasts swung grudgingly off to the flank and retreated slowly toward the watching

group on the crest. The first also tried to retreat, but another missile hit it again on the
head and it fell. Kong roared in triumph and
beat his breast.

"We'll have to get out of this," Driscoll said.
"Creep back through the bushes."

Off to the right, through a fringe of trees,
could be seen the rocky edge of a narrow,
stark ravine; and at one point what looked like
a fallen log led to the seeming safety of the
far side. Driscoll pointed, and they all began
sliding away.

The ravine invited for a second reason.
Kong, still roaring his triumph, had picked Ann
up and was moving off. His course bent at an
angle which, it seemed to Driscoll, would carry
the beast-god around to the far side of the
ravine. Only by crossing on the log bridge
could they keep in touch.

At first it seemed that the surviving triceratops would pass them by. It was some distance
away. It, too, had been struck by more than
one of Kong's asphalt slabs and had suffered
injuries which held the center of its thoughts.

"Keep down!" Denham repeated Driscoll's
warning.

They got a little closer to the trees.

Suddenly, without reason, the triceratops
wheeled at right angles to its line of retreat
and lumbered toward them. They dared not
risk the chance that it would turn again be-

fore seeing them. All leaped erect and fled. And again, as with the dinosaur, all got clear except the slowest man. Glancing back in fright, this one crashed into a low-hanging branch, fell, and picked himself up too late. He tried to swing behind the shelter of a small tree but the blundering triceratops crashed into this and came down in a heap, man and tree underneath. Then, as the others watched, the beast rose on its foreknees, felt for its victim with its long central horn, and gored him to death.

Chapter 12

Stumbling toward the ravine, the weary survivors of the searching party showed none of
the confidence which had been so high in them
when they trotted away from the great gate.
They were picked men. Every one had been
proved more than ordinarily resourceful. Again
and again when confronted with sudden danger they had revealed and sustained the high
courage which is the adventurer's final salva-
tion, more potent than any weapon. Cast away
in any ordinary wilderness they would have
boldly combined their wisdom and ingenuity
and won out. But here, for the first time, they
knew the meaning of utter helplessness. Of
what use was such guile and wit as theirs

against the huge fantastic beasts of this night-
mare island? Their frail knives, too, were useless. As they ran it was borne home upon them
that along with their rifles and bombs had sunk
their last hope. Armed with these they could
have fought on. Lacking them they were as
helpless as the trapped triceratops and its mate
slowly smothering to death back in the morass.
No one, not even the buoyant Jimmy, stood
ready now to say that the odds were fifty-fifty.

Hard, sullen oaths dropped from their lips
as they ran; not oaths of defiance, but the bitter, resentful bursts of men who have been en-
meshed through no fault of their own and who
see no way of escape.

Only Driscoll and Denham fought against
this mood of surrender. Leading the tired flight
the young mate cudgeled his brain for the
trick which would help his weaponless hands
to free Ann from her strange captor. Trailing
in second place Denham ordered his wits to
call up a picture of the trail they had taken
out from the village. They must go back, if
they could. One man must stay and try to keep
track of Kong; but the others must go back for
more rifles, more bombs. Then they would have
a chance.

From the rear came the crash of a heavy
body ploughing among the trees.

"That damned three-horned brute is hunting
us," one of the crew called out.

"Wait, Jack!" Denham said as Driscoll started across the log. "We've got a minute. The triceratops can't cross after us. And we've got to talk."

He sketched his plan in as few words as he could manage.

"Right!" Driscoll agreed. "I'll stay. You go for the guns and bombs."

"You'd better get across the ravine," Denham said. "But we won't cross unless we have to. If that brute back of us will only get it into his crazy head that we aren't the ones who hurt him we'll be saved a big walk."

As Driscoll started across the giant log Denham looked down. The ravine was very deep, with a thick deposit of mud and slime at the bottom. Alongside this reeking deposit, and indeed all the way up the steep sides, were narrow mouthed caves and long, jagged fissures in the rock. Denham looked up from all this to watch Driscoll's progress with silent anxiety. He sighed when the mate got across.

"Good boy!" he called. "I'd have felt funny, Jack, if you had started to slip. That place down there is the breeding spot for the rottenest thing on this foul island. Look!"

As though exorcised by his pointing finger, a spider like a keg on many legs came crawling out of a cave. It may not have been aware of the watchers on the high margin of the ravine, but every one would have sworn the thing stared up malevolently. Something which would have been a lizard except for its size lay warming itself on a sunny ledge. The spider moved toward it, then thought better of the impulse and looked about for smaller prey. This was provided by a round, crawling object with tentacles like those of an octopus. The spider crawled to the attack. Both octopus-insect and spider vanished into a fissure.

"I'm not going to cross that log with those things under me," a sailor announced.

Denham looked back. The triceratops, in its short-sighted fashion, was blundering about at the edge of the trees. It had taken some time to lurch through the narrow woods, and now did not seem to know which way to go.

"Maybe we won't have to," he said. "Stand fast. If we don't move, that half-blind brute may think we're rocks or tree trunks."

The triceratops broke past the last of the trees, moved uncertainly and finally began a slow advance, its great horned head lifted high, its deep-set eyes peering forward.

"That settles it," Denham said reluctantly. "We'll have to cross."

Obedient to his motioning hand, the men moved out on to the long bridge. They moved cautiously, because of what crawled far below their uncertain feet. Hurrying them as much as he could, Denham looked back at the triceratops, picked up a rock and then threw the useless thing away. The men were grouped

Ann is held by the natives.

Kong breaks through the gate into the village.

Denham displays the mighty Kong to New York City.

Previously unreleased photograph!

Ann in Kong's grasp.

Atop the Empire State Building, Kong bats away fighter planes.

Previously unreleased photograph!

close together in the center of the log, advancing slowly. Denham stepped forward.

"Look out!"

On the opposite side Driscoll stood motioning frantically toward the ground sloping behind him. He motioned again, and with a last shout caught a vine at the edge of the ravine, swung down to a ledge and flung himself into a shallow cave.

Kong came lumbering up the slope, and at sight of the men on the log roared out and beat his chest. Stopping at a lightning-riven tree he placed Ann's unconscious form in a notch as high up as his great arms could reach and then lunged forward to attack this new enemy so unexpectedly appearing to threaten possession of his bright-haired prize. Still angry from his earlier fight with the triceratopses, he was doubly enraged now by the men. And at the further sight of the three-horned beast charging toward the ravine his rage broke all bounds.

Denham followed Driscoll's example and slid over the edge of the ravine into a fissure on his side. The men on the log could do nothing. To advance against Kong was impossible. To retreat was no less so, for the triceratops, sighting his old foe, rushed up to the end of the log and bellowed a challenge. Denham and Driscoll, from their caves, watched the tragedy helplessly.

To Kong all moving beings in his vision were enemies, the men on the log as much as the beast behind it. He roared and beat his breast again. One of his great hand-like feet reached out as though he meant to attack at close quarters. At that moment a maddened plunge of the triceratops brought the beast jarringly against its end of the bridge. The men in the center clung frantically. The beast-god gave his own end of the log an experimental shake, and when the men cried out and clung to the bark, to one another, he began to chatter.

Driscoll, from his cave, shouted menacingly. Kong caught sight of him, took a half step away from the log, but in the end refused to be diverted. Denham tried the effect of a rock, but that went unnoticed. Ignoring shouts and rocks, ignoring even the bellowed defiance of the triceratops, Kong curved both forearms under his end of the log and straining upward got it off the ground and jerked it violently from side to side.

Two of the men lost their holds. One grasped madly at the face of a prone comrade and left bloody finger marks as he went whirling down into the decaying silt at the bottom. He had no more than struck when the lizard flashed upon him. Driscoll, watching, hoped that the complete lack of movement meant unconsciousness, or, better, that death had come immediately. The second man did not die in the fall. He was not even unconscious. He landed feet first, sinking immediately to his waistline in the mud, and screamed horribly as not one but half a dozen of the great spiders swarmed over him.

Up on the edge of the ravine the triceratops stamped the ground. Getting no notice from his adversary across the gap he bellowed uncertainly and began backing up. With a last bellow he wheeled around and lumbered toward the trees.

Kong lifted the log and jerked it again. Another man fell, prey for a new outpouring of spiders. Another jerk, and the octopus-insect, along with a score of companions, began to fight against the spiders and the lizards for the booty. Only one man was left on the log and he clung desperately. Kong jerked, but could not shake him loose. Nor could all the despairing efforts of Driscoll and Denham, all their shouts, all their rocks, turn the beast-god from his purpose. The clinging man shrieked. Kong glowered down upon him and in a culminating exasperation swung the log far sideways and dropped it. The end caught on the very edge of the ravine and then slipped slowly off to drop like a battering ram upon the insects at their feast below.

Driscoll, looking down in horror, found himself menaced. A spider was climbing the heavy vine which hung in front of the cave and by means of which the mate had got over the edge of the ravine. Its lidless, protruding eyes of no describable color looked up unblinkingly. Driscoll drew his knife and hacked desperately. Before the vine parted the spider had got so close that its soft exhalation was audible to the mate as it plunged back into the ravine, reaching futilely at other vines.

Cold and shaking from the tragedy he had witnessed and had been unable to avert, Driscoll nevertheless put his mind to the rescue of Ann.

"You go along," he called to Denham, "I'll stay here until that hairy brute clears out and then I'll follow him. You come back with bombs and something to bridge the ravine. I'll try to mark a plain trail."

"I feel rotten, leaving you," Denham shouted back.

"It's the one chance. Shove off!" Driscoll called impatiently.

He was so intent upon speeding Denham's departure that he was not aware of Kong's great questing hand until the director shouted a warning.

The beast-god had come to squat at the edge of the ravine and feel down into the cave for this other of his enemies. Driscoll backed up, and drawing his knife, stabbed shrewdly into Kong's dusty, hairless palm. The beast-god jerked away and roared. Denham threw a rock. Kong brushed the spot on his breast where the missile had struck and groped down again into the cave.

This time he snatched quickly, missed and got clear. He snatched again, and again missed. Enraged, he thrust his hand deep into the cave and began a slow groping search. Driscoll stabbed, but the beast-god ignored the wounds. He ignored Denham's rocks, too.

Driscoll crouched in his shallow wall, stabbing hopelessly at every chance. Twice the huge, curving fingers touched him; twice he dug his knife in and got away. Now he was in a corner from which the swinging hand barred escape. If he could cut the tendons at wrist or elbow, he might gain at least a moment. Crouching lower, making himself as small as possible, he gripped his knife and watched for an opening. . . .

Chapter 13

The vague hurt of the riven branch grew to
sharp pain as Ann came back to consciousness.
She turned on one side and the wall of the
notch in which she lay met her eyes. Looking
up from that, she saw only the sky. Where she
was, she had not the dimmest notion, and for
a moment she could remember nothing. She
was bruised, and shaken, and a pall of stark
fear hung over her, but beyond that her brain
refused to go. Almost ready to drop back into
unconsciousness, she rested on her rough support and by a complete lack of motion soothed
her racked body.

Then, abruptly, a black apelike horror filled
her mind and she sat up screaming. Nothing

was forgotten now. She recalled the smallest details. The especially bright flame of one torch as she had stood bound upon the altar; the red eyes which had burned down upon her for one instant, closed and burned again; the great furry hand which had reached out at first so doubtfully; the hairy corded shoulder upon which she had lain in the moment before all consciousness faded; the recurring moments thereafter when she had felt herself being swung along through the forest.

Sitting up, she discovered where she was and had a fresh immediate cause for fright. She dared not jump. The height alone was a bar but besides that, at the base of her tree, crawled a snake whose head swayed up along the trunk. Moreover, there was Kong.

Kong crouched at the brink of a ravine. His great bulk rested on strong haunches while a long, black arm swung over the edge and groped persistently. In addition to Kong there was a third living thing.

Out from the bushes which covered the slope below Ann's perch came a grotesque, hopping creature of very little less than Kong's own bulk. Its long slender neck scouted hungrily in every direction as it progressed upon powerful hind legs. Of forelegs it had almost none; only frail, clawlike members good for nothing save to lift food to its mouth. It was the mouth which caused Ann to scream again.

Nothing she had seen was quite so horrible as that red aperture filled with pointed carnivorous teeth; and when the long neck swung in her direction she thought she was lost.

At her scream Kong whirled about. The snake, sliding off hurriedly, got a cuff in passing, but all the beast-god's fury broke upon the huge meat-eater. Clenched hands beating a tattoo upon his deep breast, Kong lumbered to the attack.

The meat-eater stood ground defiantly and as Kong drew close flicked out its snakelike head, teeth bared and gleaming. Kong swept the head aside and plunged in. Both creatures fell off their balance. Kong was on top and for a moment it seemed that the fight was to be finished instantly. The slim swaying neck was far too fragile to withstand for long the powerful hands closed about it. But before Kong could make his grip sure the meat-eater squeezed one thick hind leg up against his assailant's breast and thrust. Not even Kong's strength could hold on against the force of that drive. His hand grip was broken and he whirled backward, head over heels, to the brink of the ravine.

"No!" Ann cried out. "No! No!"

She wanted Kong to win. She had no thought that she could survive much longer the horror of captivity in his hands, but even that was preferable to the open mouth which briefly swung her way before it flicked out again to meet Kong's renewed attack.

The beast-god lumbered back, beating his breast and indifferent to all his enemy's blows. His roaring charge carried both fighters hard against the tree in which Ann crouched and that long-tormented pedestal crashed down. Stunned by the fall, Ann lay under the main trunk. That was barely held away from her by a short spike of branch. On top of the tree, Kong and his adversary writhed until a deadly hind foot parted them again.

The beast-god moved back promptly, but now he spent less time beating his breast to terrify an enemy which would not be terrified by such devices. He came in more deliberately. Any critical observer would have realized that Kong had met enemies of the meat-eater breed before and had worked out a technique of battle which served well when he was not too enraged to use it. Now, at last, his rage was in check. His eyes always upon the long flicking neck, he came in purposefully and at last reached, not for the head but for one of the frail forelegs. He twisted it furiously and leaped away as the meat-eater bit into his shoulder. Again he was in and again away. This time the attacked foreleg hung limp and the meat-eater was in unmistakable distress. Now Kong once more dared a frontal attack. As at first he plunged recklessly forward and fastened his black hands upon the darting neck. As before the two fell in a heap and a great hind leg thrust against Kong's chest.

This time, however, the co-ordination was not so perfect; the force was less, and as he went whirling back Kong was able to seize the foot which drove him. That was the major advantage he had been seeking. The extended leg had so little power that he was able to twist it and spin the meat-eater over onto its stomach. In a flash Kong leaped astride his enemy's back. His knees clamped about the narrow shoulders. His great hands reached up to snatch at the open mouth. Before the meat-eater could use the powerful leverage of its hind legs to shake off its rider, the hands found their objective. They closed upon the upper and lower jaw and pulled. Nothing could have withstood such fury. The meat-eater's mouth gave in either direction and Kong leaped clear. Battering his breast exultantly, he roared and gibbered his triumph while his foe rolled and threshed upon the ground in weaker and weaker convulsions.

When the meat-eater finally stretched out in death, Kong drew close and gazed down with loud cheeps of pleasure. He waggled the broken jaws with satisfaction and looked over toward Ann as though to invite her praise. Ann, however, could indicate neither praise nor horror. Her over-taxed emotions had once

more sent her into unconsciousness. Trapped
by the trunk which stood barely clear of her
curving breast, she lay as motionless as the
great creature Kong had killed.

Driscoll lifted his head half above the margin of the ravine to watch. He could scarcely
contain himself when Kong lumbered over and
touched Ann solicitiously. But he had reasoned
his course out and he stood by it. Ann had
come unhurt so far. Her one chance for continued safety depended upon his own ability
to keep track of her and upon Kong's temper.
If he managed to trail the beast-god, and if
he did not provoke him to a furious outburst,
Ann might be saved by the party Denham was
to bring back.

Driscoll was the more inclined to keep quiet
because of his growing conviction that Kong
had completely forgotten him. The ape-like
creature did not make a single motion back
toward the cave. With all his interest focused
upon Ann, he curved his arms about the tree
as he had curved them about the bridge log.
Carefully, by deliberate inches, he lifted the
great weight and swung it to one side. Only
when it was clear of Ann did he lower it back
to the ground, and then as gently as he had
lifted it; and when the heavy tree-trunk was
carried aside he lumbered back anxiously. As
he raised Ann, his broad throat made curious
consoling sounds. Carefully, and as easily as a

man might have raised a doll, he rested his prize against a shoulder and turned down the slope.

Driscoll, behind the edge of the ravine, sensed a clear purpose back of the departure. Freed at last of all pursuit, victorious over the last of a succession of enemies, Kong, the mate felt sure, was going directly now to the home he had not been able to reach before. No longer fretted by the small noisy man-things who had trailed him from the altar, safely past the morass into which the triceratops had driven him, and secure from the hungry pursuit of the man-eater, he was bearing his prize home.

Driscoll clambered cautiously to firm ground. Advancing a little he made sure of Kong's line of flight and no less sure that it was not too fast for him to keep up with. Then he turned around and looked for Denham. The latter was up on the far side of the bank, waiting. At his feet lay a great coil of vine rope. He grinned down at it.

"I got it ready while the fight was on," he said. "I figured that if Kong lost, maybe you could get Ann, and I could get one end of this to you, and we could do something."

For the first time since he had left the village, Driscoll felt a surge of the old affection for his employer. Denham was, and no doubt about it, a man you could tie to. He got you

into trouble, plenty. But he never stopped trying to get you out.

"The stuff may come in handy yet," he
agreed, and smiled. "Leave it right there. And
you shove back to the village."

"I hate like hell to leave you, Jack."

"What else can you do?" Driscoll asked.
"The two of us can't catch Kong. We've got
to have bombs to do that. You go get them. I'll
mark the trail from here. And we'll save Ann
as sure as anything you know."

"I guess that's the only way out."

"Sure it is."

Denham stood looking at the resolute young
face across the ravine.

"O.K., Jack. Good luck!" he said and wheel-
ing around went back at a trot toward the
stream from which the dinosaur had pursued
them.

"See you later—maybe," Driscoll called, and
waved goodbye, as Denham vanished into the
woods.

A distant crashing sounded in the heavy
brush far down the slope. Driscoll nodded.
That would be Kong, headed for his hide-
away. Close to the tree in which Ann had
rested, lay the meat-eater's body. Already vul-
tures were on the thing, half a dozen of them,
and more were coming. From over the edge of
the ravine the sharp reptilian head of a giant
lizard announced that the scent of fresh food

had drifted deep down to the hungry things which lived in the slime below. Driscoll shivered and went gladly on the trail of his larger enemy.

Chapter 14

The brush which grew thick upon the Plain of the Altar rose more often than not above Denham's waist as he dragged his weary feet along. Sometimes when it grew especially tall, or when he bent in a moment of unusual fatigue, it concealed him entirely. Night was well forward, too. A dozen factors made his slow-moving, exhausted figure hard to pick up, even from the high vantage point of the wall. Sharp eyes, however, were watching. The smoky flames of torches marked the niche where a dozen sailors kept vigilant guard down by the gate, ready to pull its great doors wide. Other torches, flickering on high, told of more men leaning forward to peer from the rampart. And one of these last sighted the solitary walker

long before he got to the cleared ground
around the altar.

"Yo-ho! Denham!"

It was Englehorn who called. His white cap
swung dimly in a wide encouraging circle. The
torches became trailing arcs of flame as the
crew joined in the shout.

"Yo-ho-o-o-o! Yo-ho-o-o-o, away there!"

The figures on the wall vanished, reappear-
ing almost at once to swell the ranks at the
gate. The gate swung wide, and the loud shout
rang on until Denham had struggled through
the last fringe of brush and had slogged past
the altar. Then, however, silence fell, as
abruptly as the shout had risen. The whole
group at the gate stood taut, gazing in bewilderment over Denham's head when the
darkness there failed to reveal any others following.

Englehorn recovered first. Dropping his
torch, he ran out and got an arm under Denham's sagging shoulders.

"I've got you," he murmured, and all but
carried his friend to a bench inside the gate.

"Where are the others?" a sailor wanted to
know.

"Let that wait!" Englehorn ordered brus-
quely. "Get some whiskey and some food. And
close the gate."

"No!" Denham cut in. "Leave the gate open.
If Driscoll comes, he'll come in a hurry."

"Where is Driscoll?"

"Where's Miss Ann?" Lumpy added.

"I said, let that wait," Englehorn emphasized. "Where's the whiskey?"

While the bottle stood tilted against Denham's mouth, the eyes of the skipper and the rest searched his torn clothing, his cut and bruised flesh, his grey face. They waited fearfully for a beginning of the dark account of adventure they felt was impending.

Englehorn did not move the bottle until the liquor had dropped to an imaginary line drawn by a generously measuring thumb. With the final swallow, Denham shuddered, and wiping his mouth slowly with the back of his hand leaned against the captain's hard thigh.

"I could do with that grub you spoke of," he said.

Englehorn nodded and cocked a commanding eye. The man he picked out went reluctantly. He half swung back as the others crowded around for Denham's next word, but Englehorn's sharp, "Shove along!" kept him going.

Denham straightened on his bench as the whiskey took hold and faced his crew squarely.

"Well!" he said. "There's no use trying to give it to you softly. Here's the story. Everyone's wiped out, except Driscoll and possibly Ann. And I'm asking for volunteers to go back after them. Who is coming with me?"

His audience, eyes shining under the smoky torches, gazed down uncomprehendingly.

"What do you mean, wiped out?"

"You mean something's happened?"

"I mean . . ." The words caught in his throat and Denham stopped to swallow. "I mean wiped out," he plunged on. "Wait till I tell you what we ran into.

"That black, hairy brute you saw go off with Miss Darrow is only the beginning of what this hell-made island has to offer. And the men I took out last night didn't miss anything."

He paused, to order his mind, and then told them as briefly as a profound sense of responsibility would let him what had happened. Reaching the tragic crisis upon the log bridge he gave every detail.

"I want you to know just what you'll be up against," he said, "when you decide to go back with me."

"I ain't sure I get it all," one of the sailors said. "How . . ." he ended lamely in a mumble of words.

"You want to know how I got clear?" Denham asked. "Is that it? How I and Driscoll got away?" His nod of agreement had all his normal tolerance, as he set out patiently to explain the happenstance which had placed him in a position to leap to safety, and Driscoll in one of equal advantage while the rest were trapped between the triceratops and Kong.

"I don't mean to claim any credit," he emphasized. "If I had kept a proper eye on the bombs we'd all be safe, including Miss Darrow. But just the same it was because I was trying to see the others safely across that I happened to be off the log. And as for Driscoll, at the time he went over to the far side of the ravine, he was taking a far bigger risk than anyone who stayed behind."

The man who had put the question nodded solemnly, and the others were plainly in agreement.

"You couldn't have helped what happened," Englehorn murmured. "No matter what you did."

"Not a nickel's worth," Denham said confidently. "I'll tell you the truth. I'll never forget I was the one to take them into it. But nobody can say I let them down. And if I weren't here now, Driscoll and Ann wouldn't have a Chinaman's chance."

"We'll never see them again," Lumpy declared blackly.

"The hell we won't!" Denham shouted, and stood up. "We'll see 'em both. And quick! Skipper, I want a case of bombs fetched. I'm backtrailing on the jump." He looked around and repeated his earlier question. "Who is coming with me?"

"Lemme go, Mr. Denham," Lumpy begged. "If I can't get stouter, younger men, you can go and welcome," Denham said frankly. He looked up at the others. "How about it?"

The whole lot of them stepped forward in a confusion of assent . . . casual, reckless, indifferent or jovial, according as each man reacted to the sharp stimulant of danger.

"I'll string along."

"Hell's bells! Why not?"

"Seein' it don't cost anything."

"Might as well."

"I guess I owe the mate this one."

"Miss Ann sewed some buttons on my shirt once."

Having had their say, their faces fell into a common sobriety. They had no illusions about what they would face if they went out, and as they remembered what had happened to their comrades their humor and bravado died away.

Englehorn was among the volunteers, along with a persistent Lumpy, but Denham waved these two back.

"I've got enough without you," he said to Lumpy, "and as for you, Skipper, you draw the same billet. You stay here and keep the gate."

"I'm fresher than you," Englehorn pointed out.

"But I know the trail."

"You could draw me a map."

"Skipper! I wouldn't let the freshest man in all the Indian Ocean take my place," Denham said wryly. "Not even if he was the best map reader in the seven seas."

"I wouldn't either, in your shoes, Mr. Denham," the skipper responded with understanding heartiness.

Denham nodded, and turned to the food the commandeered cook had brought up. As he ate, he gave his orders.

"Get me a rifle," he directed, "and a full bandolier. Every other man take the same. A knife apiece, too. There'll be a dozen bombs in the box when it comes up. Six of you take two apiece. And remember! All the hell we drew on the first trip came because neither I nor anyone else had sense enough to hang onto a couple of bombs. Don't you lads lose yours."

"You think the bombs will stop those big brutes you told us about?" a sailor asked.

The other waited expectantly.

"Stop them?" Denham laughed. "Just one will stop the biggest of the lot in his tracks. Even Kong." And in proof he retold in detail how the first huge enemy had been halted and brought down.

"When do you plan to start?" Englehorn wanted to know.

"Now! On the dot."

"Too soon, Mr. Denham," the skipper murmured. After his first shock and concern, he was chewing tobacco again in his customary placid thoughtfulness.

"This second wouldn't be too soon."

"Figure it out, Mr. Denham. If you go now, you'll get to the ravine long before dawn. And then what can you do? Nothing but sit around to be picked off by whatever comes along until you can see to follow Driscoll's trail."

Denham hurriedly thought out a time schedule and then he nodded in reluctant agreement.

"But how I can sit around here, waiting, for almost four hours is more than I know."

"Call in their ringleader, that witch doctor," Lumpy suggested malevolently. "He ought to be able to get us some tips. And if he won't, I know ways we can make him."

"Where is he?"

Englehorn hadn't seen either the witch doctor or the chief for hours. Nor had any of the others.

"I knocked the chief cold just after you and Driscoll started off," he explained placidly. "With the butt of his own spear. Because he acted as though he was going to follow and stop you. And after I did that the whole tribe seemed to get low in the mouth. I got the idea they felt trouble was coming and wanted to get as far away as possible."

"I wonder where they could have gone?" Denham puzzled.

"I think a lot of the women are still in the

huts. We've all heard sounds now and then. And as for the men! Well, this part of the island back of the wall is pretty big; and covered with brush. Hiding in it wouldn't be very hard."

"You don't think they're planning a surprise attack, do you?"

"Not if I know natives," Englehorn said confidently. "And I think I know 'em pretty well. The truth is, they don't think they need to attack us themselves. They figure Kong'll do it for them. We've been pretty high-handed, first refusing Kong a sacrifice and then chasing him after he got one. Knowing Kong, they think we can't do such things without paying. And they think it'll be Kong who will be back to collect. And when he does they want to be as far away as possible."

"By the Lord!" Denham cried softly. "They're right! Kong *will* be back. At least he will if we manage to recapture Ann."

The sailors, busy with their rifles and knives, looked up in a total lack of comprehension. Even Englehorn was puzzled, and after chewing a while he said so.

"I don't see why. It seems to me he'll more likely be hunting something to eat."

Denham, clinging doggedly to the theory he had revealed to Driscoll, shook his head.

"Kong," he insisted, "is the one thing outside the wall that is something more than beast. He's one of nature's errors, like all the others, but he was nearly not an error. And in that huge head of his is a spark. Ann means something to him."

Englehorn made a doubtful sound.

"Yes, she does," Denham declared. "If I didn't believe that I wouldn't have a solitary hope of seeing her again. You don't suppose he took such care of the native girls they tied to the altar, do you?"

Englehorn conceded that Kong probably hadn't. He had gathered in his brief talk with the chief that the natives had been surprised when Kong carried Ann with such care into the dark shadow of the precipice.

"He sensed that Ann was different," Denham said, seizing upon the skipper's concession. "He hadn't the faintest notion why she is different. And he doesn't in the least know what to do with her. But when he looked on her something inside him gave way. It was Beauty and the Beast all over again."

Speaking solely to Englehorn . . . as a matter of fact, the sailors, after listening for a little in perplexity, had shaken their heads and pushed forward their preparations for the hunt . . . Denham once again outlined his theory of how Beauty softens and attracts and in the end encompasses the destruction of the Beast.

"He'll lose Ann in the end," Denham said.

"One way or another. And after he does, he'll never again be quite the same king of the forest. Brute strength will have yielded to something higher, and by the extent of its yielding will be weakened for its future battles with other brutes."

"A very pretty theory," Englehorn murmured, "but in my opinion, Mr. Denham, it isn't worth the rust on a single hull plate. It's moon talk and nothing more. Kong was attracted by Ann's bright head, I'll grant you. But only because it was strange. Only as a magpie is attracted by a shining stone. And he'll tire of her brightness just as the magpie does. When he gets hungry he'll drop Ann. And my prayer is that when he does, Driscoll will be there to pick her up."

"We can trust Jack," Denham said confidently. He looked at his watch. "I wish to heaven it was time for me to do my share."

Chapter 15

Kong was following no beaten trail; but he left his great tracks plainly upon bruised leaves, and broken branches, and sodden jungle floor. Driscoll had far less difficulty in pursuing him than he had anticipated. Even without the telltale marks he would have been seldom puzzled. Kong bothered so little about the noise he made that the crash of his heavy progress was often a guiding echo through the thick wood. It helped, too, that his gait was leisurely. He seemed in no hurry at all; and if there were enemies about he certainly did not seem to fear them.

Only one aspect of the beast-god's march indicated that the district might not be as empty of dangers as it appeared. This was the fact that he travelled by no well-defined paths. All along the way there were crossing and criss-crossing of trails which could have belonged only to the great creatures of the incredible island. But Kong broke a way through virgin jungle. He used no old path which his enemies could have come to know.

Driscoll found the pursuit so easy that on occasion he misjudged his own speed and got too close. He always had a moment of panic when this happened, and he had to swerve hastily for cover. He was still convinced that his one hope of rescuing Ann, either by himself or by keeping contact until a larger rescuing party caught up, depended upon his success in arousing no suspicion of pursuit. If Kong discovered he was being followed, anything might happen. So Driscoll kept well back, following by sound rather than by sight.

Around noon, despite his care, he emerged into one border of a clearing as Kong disappeared on the other. And because he had been so long without any reassuring glimpse, he risked the briefest of inspections.

Ann was, apparently, still unconscious. He prayed that she was not merely motionless from fright. In any event she made no movement while Driscoll had her in view. Even one drooping arm seemed utterly without life. She lay in the crook of one of the beast-god's enormous arms. She might have been in a swing-seat she rode so easily, the curved prop giving with every stride and every shift of Kong's loose-jointed body. The last pin had fallen from her hair and it foamed down her back in a bright cascade made more bright by its contrast with Kong's black snarl of fur. One sleeve of her dress had been torn, so that her right shoulder was bare. The soft, white rondure made another, more startling contrast with her captor's sooty bulk.

The clearing proved to be the beginning of thinner vegetation. The trail, which had led for a time gently downward from the crest of the ravine, sloped up again. Gradually the tangle of vines and lush undergrowth disappeared. The trees, taller now, stood by themselves with no cluttering brush at their roots. By mid-afternoon Driscoll began to catch glimpses of the tip of Skull Mountain. And by that time Kong's purposeful travel made it additionally plain that he was on his way to his lair.

That lair could be nowhere except up the slope of the island's highest peak, Driscoll reasoned; some fastness accessible only to a mighty climber. Such a spot, far from the vegetation which nourished most of the other beasts, would be doubly attractive since it would have no attraction to draw the rarer, meat-eating creatures. The likelihood of all this became more evident as the curious pursuit continued, the dogged man-animal clinging to the trail of an enemy twenty times as large.

Toward twilight the chase led more steeply upward through a boulder-strewn region, and Driscoll tired rapidly. His body throbbed from falls and blows of branches; he was hungry, besides; and his feet and legs were numb from exhaustion as he stumbled along after the sounds Kong made.

It was only tardily that he noted a phenomenon which confronted him after one long swing to the left. This was a great spout of water bursting from the very side of the mountain itself. A white, misty, torrent, it had dug a deep pit under its point of egress and from this it spilled into a narrow channel to tumble down and disapper into the jungle below.

Upon Driscoll's mind, grown hard from fatigue, the existence of this stream made at first only the faintest of marks. A stream! But the mark deepened as it came to him that this might well be the beginning of the stream which far back widened into the lagoon of the dinosaur, and which still farther poured softly over that slide leading down to the Plain of the Altar. He was contemplating this possibility when he rounded a jutting corner of rock and discovered Kong scarcely a hundred yards ahead and in full view.

Only a frantic speed which brought an

added protest from his tired muscles got him
back behind the shield of rock in time.

Peering out from his hiding place he saw
that Kong had come to a full stop in a great,
natural amphitheater which was encircled in
three-quarters of its circumference by a curving cliff. A broad black pool lay just forward
of the beast-god, and at this he was staring
with greater and greater suspicion. It was a
curious pool, as still as it was black, and seemingly without any source. At one point it came
to within a few feet of the base of the cliff.
High up on this last a ledge ran, and at one
place the ledge broadened to make a wide platform before a cave.

Nowhere was there any sign of flowing water
which fed the pool. On the contrary, on the
side unfettered by wall, Driscoll caught sight
of a whirling movement which could mean
only an outlet. An underground outlet of con-
siderable size, too. The mystery broke clear for
him then, and simultaneously he realized that
his conclusion about the spout of water seen
earlier had been only half right. The spout
was one beginning of the stream, but not the
beginning. That was here, in the black, still
pool. From somewhere, doubtless from a source
far below in the ocean's bed, this water welled
up to the pool. There, through the ages, it had
eaten away a fault in the rock to make a sub-

terranean passage. By this it broke at last through the mountain's side.

Why Kong should stare suspiciously at this pool, Driscoll could not imagine; and he was all the more puzzled as he remembered the cave on the high ledge and the full significance of this dawned. For the cave was in a dead-end path. There was no road beyond the pool. If Kong wished to leave he must go by the way he had come. And this could mean only one thing. Kong was home. The cave was his lair. And since it was his lair, the spot must be familiar to him. So, Driscoll pondered, why should the ape-beast be suspicious?

Puzzled, he peered around his jutting rock. Then he saw the cause of Kong's delay. What had before seemed an added blackness in the deepening evening light became a solid something, a crawling bulk whose upraised head faced Kong on the rocky margin while its serpentine length disappeared into the pool.

Kong crouched as the thing twisted farther out of the pool. He gave back a few steps to drop Ann roughly at the base of the cliff. Leaping forward again he stood erect and rolled out his deep challenge.

Driscoll had never thought to hear that thunder of rage without terror. But when it beat upon his ears, with its accompanying tattoo of mighty hands upon mighty chest, he was no more than a breath away from a sup-

porting shout. He had never thought to see
Kong barring the way to Ann with any emotion save hate. But when the crouching ape-
beast swung before the white shoulder which
marked Ann's place against the dark rock the
mate could have cried out in thanks.

Roaring, Kong charged in to battle. Somewhere, upon a rock at the bottom of the pool,
the monster's tail had taken hold and this gave
it added strength to meet Kong's rush. Kong
fought with hands and long, flashing teeth.
Even more than these his feet were factors.
They gripped the uneven rocks and withstood
the tug of the submerged tail as the monster
coiled around the beast-god's pillar-like legs
and tried to slip back into the pool.

Unlike Kong's earlier conflicts this was a
silent fight. The water beast had no voice and
Kong, after the first roar which announced
his assault, had breath only for an occasional
enraged whimper. His teeth slashed at the
crushing coils and his hands struggled to hold
the monster's head.

Driscoll, watching from behind his corner
of rock, could see no advantage on either side
for long minutes. The coils seemed to bind as
terribly as ever. Kong's teeth slashed unrelent-
ingly, and his hands still fought the monster's
swinging head. When the end did come it
came so suddenly that Driscoll had no warning. Kong dropped into a slightly lower crouch,

his legs spraddled a little more widely apart,
his arms snatched the monstrous head close
against his deep breast. That was all. But in
that all but imperceptible series of efforts were
both the seed and the fruit of another victory
for the beast king who dominated the lost
world of Skull Mountain Island. The water
boiled as the monster's tail let go in agony.
The huge coils dropped to make a writhing
rest for the crushed head which Kong flung
down.

Kong swayed and all but fell. He was so
drained of breath and strength that for a space
he could not even step outside the twisted
mound of flesh which still encircled his feet.
He shivered, so full he was of the loathing his
species has had of reptilian things since the
dawn of time, but he was too spent to move.
And when he had recovered enough to raise
Ann once more to the crook of his arm and
toil slowly up to the ledge and his lofty cave,
he was still too stupefied from his struggle to
look around for any other danger.

For the first time in the long pursuit, Driscoll felt no fear of detection. He came out
from behind his rock and, knife in hand, half
considered an attack. But he put that thought
down quickly. The great hands might have
spent their best strength upon the monster, but
they still had strength to crush him. Reluctantly, he drew back again into hiding and

prepared for what would be the hardest hours. Now, in spite of fatigue, he must keep awake to watch and listen for the rescue party; more, he must watch and listen for the moment when Ann might need him.

Where he stood was all darkness now, a safe hiding place from which to watch Kong's accent to the ledge. Slowly, by pushing foot and lifting hand, the beast-god made his way. There was no path, but each jutting rock was good for a gain of feet. Driscoll marked the course and told himself that if need be he could climb it too.

Standing finally before the cave, Kong put Ann down between his feet. As she lay there, unmoving, he drew deep breaths. His strength came back with every inhalation. His head began to weave and his arms to swing. The arms swung higher and higher, and then they were at his chest drumming in a wild ecstasy while from his swelling throat there lifted a long peal of triumph.

High above, in the star-lit sky, a great bird-like monster soared and seemed to listen. Kong redoubled his cry and flung it upward, challengingly.

Driscoll, in the darkness below, saw Ann stir and sit erect. Uncertainly, she twisted around to look up toward the voice above her. Then she screamed, as she had screamed on the Plain of the Altar.

Kong broke off his own savage speech and looked down. In the faint light Ann was now no more than a shadow except where her dress was torn. There, however, her shoulder was white and softly gleaming. Kong squatted down. His hand went first to the foaming hair which he last remembered as brightly shining. He pulled it as though puzzled that a thing could be so different, by night, from what it was by day. He fingered it, shook it off, and reached out to the inviting whiteness of the shoulder.

Ann screamed again. Kong snatched at her. His hand caught in her dress and the dress tore in his huge fingers. More whiteness was revealed. Kong touched the smooth revelation. He pulled again at the torn dress. Then, holding Ann tightly, he began to pluck her clothes away as a chimpanzee might clumsily undress a doll. As each garment came free into his hand, he felt it excitedly, plainly trying to find some connection between the frail tissue and the whiteness he had exposed.

Ann cried brokenly and Driscoll, darting out from his hiding place, began to climb up to the ledge. There had been no sign of a rescue party but he could wait no longer. His muscles were too tired to perform their usual service and he slipped again and again. Once he all but pitched back to the bottom. Breathless, he hung for a space, and then climbed again.

He was wondering dully why Kong had not heard him when, looking up, he saw the great face peering over the ledge. If the face had shown anger Driscoll would have given up hope. It showed, however, only a suspicious interest. Kong had heard something, but in the darkness he had not seen. Driscoll flattened himself against the rock and waited. Suddenly Kong's face drew back.

Driscoll struggled furiously up the last few feet. He reasoned that if he had been detected caution was useless. If, on the other hand, Kong had been diverted speed might possibly carry him to his goal before any fresh suspicion was aroused.

He pulled himself over the ledge in time to see Kong seize a great pterodactyl and begin its destruction.

This time the affair was not a fight. It was too one-sided for that. The reptile had swooped down to the white form on the ledge. Kong had turned about in time and, seizing it as its long talons reached for Ann, angrily tore the creature to pieces. It was to this more certain menace that the beast-god had been drawn from the uncertain danger indicated by the noise Driscoll had made.

Ann was unhurt. As Kong lifted the pterodactyl clear of her she rose and stumbled to the edge of the rocky platform. Driscoll risked a whisper.

"Ann," he called softly.

"Jack! Oh, Jack!"

She crept in the direction of his voice.

Behind Kong's back they caught at one another; they whispered like two children in an ogre's castle of terrors.

"Jack! I kept praying, and praying, and you didn't come!"

"I'm here now, Ann."

Holding her close he pretended an assurance which he did not feel.

"Jack! Don't let him touch me again."

He felt for his knife and told himself he could save her from that, at least.

"You won't let him touch me, will you, Jack?"

"Don't you worry, honey," he promised and then, looking down, he remembered. The pool!

"Ann!" he whispered. "We're going to . . ."

Kong had finished his latest task of destruction. Turning, he swung the remains of the carnivorous reptile over the ledge and saw the two clasped close. His throat swelled. His angry roar sounded.

"Jump, Ann!" Driscoll cried, and with his arm fast about her waist, they leaped together.

Chapter 16

The black pool poured over Ann's head and pressed her down into a warm, soundless gulf. The water was warm! She had set her teeth against a stinging chill. But the water was, actually, warm, and marvellously soothing against her unclothed flesh. It was a soft unguent, laving every bruise and long tormented muscle. Her slim body, a wavering white shadow in the black stillness, yielded to it gratefully.

Mid-air, Driscoll had cried into her ear: "Don't be afraid; and hold your breath!" She did hold her breath, and before they had got down so far that fear seized her Driscoll twisted sideways to bring their plunge to a full stop. Then they drifted upwards. His arm had remained protectingly at her waist, but as they broke the surface it withdrew and she floated alone, filling her lungs with deep, quick gasps.

"All right? Are you all right?"

Driscoll trod water at her side and blinked his eyes free of drops which trickled down from his hair.

"Yes," Ann said faintly. "I can swim. But oh, Jack! I can't believe you've really come."

"I've come all right," said Driscoll reassuringly, but he looked swiftly back toward the ledge.

Kong, because of his people's age-old distaste for water, had taken the slower way down. At that he was almost to the bottom. By hand and foot-hold he was dropping with a speed which would have landed any other creature on the rocks in a broken heap.

"Lively it is," said Driscoll in Ann's ear.

Pointing to where the water spun into the underground channel, he explained briefly what they must do.

"I'm ready," said Ann. "But please keep close to me, Jack."

"I'll be right here." He reached out a comforting hand.

Kong made a final, long leap and came down to the bottom on resilient haunches. Hands drumming, throat full of thunder, deep-set eyes ablaze and long arms already reaching, he spraddled toward the edge of the pool.

Ann gave a cry of terror.

"Dive!" Driscoll cried.

Ann answered by jack-knifing swiftly under the water. Driscoll followed, his body taking speed from powerfully threshing legs. When Ann had to break back to the surface short of the channel's mouth he flashed past her and emerged first, on the alert.

Kong had sensed their objective, or perhaps those all but hidden eyes were sharp enough to catch their shadowy, under-water flight. A roaring fury, he lumbered toward the mouth of the channel, almost near enough to stand guard, and thrust his great arms down.

"Dive!" Driscoll cried once more.

Blindly Ann jack-knifed again.

This time the distance was easily within her limits. Deep under water her white body pointed unerringly for the goal. With every movement her few torn remnants of clothing drifted slowly alongside stroking arms and legs. She had time to be glad she had sucked her lungs full, to wish she dared look back for Driscoll, to grow cold under the shadow of a hairy, reaching paw. Then, in the same instant that Jack's hand upon her heel gave notice he was following, the suction caught her.

She had presence of mind enough not to re-

sist the current rushing her along. From somewhere the memory came of a man in a book
who had survived a fall into Canadian rapids
by letting his body swing limp against every
obstacle. She. did likewise. Hands and arms
folded about her head to protect it, she made
no resistance but allowed the water to twist
her as it would.

There were, indeed, no obstructions to come
against save the circling wall of the tunnel,
and that had been worn smooth through the
centuries. Once a knee struck painfully. But
the pitch-black passage was short. Her lungs
had scarcely begun to protest against their burden of old breath before she was flashing in
a white smother of spray out of the side of
Skull Mountain. There followed a brief drop
into a churning pocket, and then she found
herself sweeping along in the soft moonlight
between sheer, rocky banks.

"Jack!"

She called loudly, her agonized fear returning with the sense of being alone. She rolled
over on her back to look for Driscoll; and there
he was, at her very side, with a quick hand
beneath her tired head. She closed her eyes
in flooding relief. Thus sightless, she felt she
was moving twice as fast as before, and the
current had seemed swift even when she could
see.

"Easy does it," Jack said at her ear. "This road takes us all the way back to the village. And we're making great time. Even if Kong follows, he has to travel overland, and it's dollars to doughnuts we beat him.

"If we don't," he ended solemnly, "he'll have to come into the water to get us; and dive deep, too."

Still drifting upon the supporting hand, Ann reached out to touch Driscoll in mute thankfulness.

"But Jack!" she cried then. "You're hurt."

"Kong!" he explained, and his mouth shaped into a hard curve of triumph under a torn forehead. "He reached for me just as I shot into the tunnel."

Ann put gentle dripping fingers alongside the hanging triangle of flesh.

"Well, my dear," she said, laughing to keep from crying. "I haven't got enough clothes left to dress a penny doll, let alone a grown girl of my height and weight. But I certainly owe you a bandage. And if you'll just nip ashore I'll find you one, and let my maidenly modesty go hang."

That was exactly the light note the adventure required. Driscoll grinned. He had been drifting on his back, too, in order the more easily to keep his supporting hand under her head. Now he swung on his side, caught her into his arms and kissed her until they both disappeared under the water. Ann came up sputtering.

"That was only partly because I couldn't help it," Driscoll told her. "The other part was to celebrate escaping."

Ann smiled at him tremulously.

She was still haunted by her night and day of terror. She knew Kong might be following. And she was so tired that she would have dropped straight down to the swift stream's rocky bottom if Driscoll's hand had not been giving its support. She was weak from hunger too; she was only beginning to realize how famished with hunger she was. And she was aware that their flight was beset by a multitude of dangers. But she was glad, to the core of her heart.

With her eyes she called Driscoll back, and when he came close she curved an arm about his neck and kissed him lightly on the mouth.

"I want to celebrate too," she said. "And besides, I couldn't help it, either."

Driscoll kissed her a third time, but then he hauled away until he touched her only with that one hand beneath her head. In the moonlight his figure made a dark shaft apart from her drifting white shadow.

"Neither of us," he told her, "has so much as a lick of sense."

"It's nicer to be happy than sensible any day. Or night," Ann added, eyeing the moon.

"Have you," he demanded, "the faintest idea about where we are, or where we're going?"

"Wherever you say."

"Your confidence is a compliment, all right enough. But wait until I tell you a few things."

Gliding along, he explained his theory about the stream, and where he believed it led. As he talked, the bank on either side drew more deeply into shadow, and the current seemed to grow a little less strong.

"The minute you feel rested," he said, "I want you to swim. Not hard. Just enough to help the current. I don't think we have so very far to go, but we can't waste any time."

"I can swim now," Ann told him. "At least for a while."

She flashed over in the moonlight and began stroking valiantly.

"Take it easy," Driscoll cautioned. "Long ones and slow ones. All you have to do is help the current just a little."

Beneath the murky cloak of one bank's shadow Ann's arms and legs moved rhythmically in obedience to his order.

"That's fine. If you get too tired we can find a log along the shore I guess. But we'd go slower with a log. And I want to make speed. God alone knows what we're likely to meet."

"I can keep on for a while."

"We'll have to leave the water when we reach the lagoon where we found the dinosaur. No current there at all, or scarcely. We can walk around it faster than we can swim through."

At the protest of walking Ann realized her weakness and forced herself to confess it.

"I can drift along like this," she told Driscoll, "especially when you give me a hand now and then. But Jack! I couldn't walk even a hundred feet fast enough to outdistance a snail."

"I hadn't thought you could. Honey, I'm going to carry you."

"Carry! After all you've been through! Jack! You never could."

Driscoll stroked along for a little, then he said softly:

"Don't make any mistake! I could carry you ten miles if I had to."

Or, Ann said to herself, go down trying. He hadn't, she knew, the strength to carry her. Not after his night and day of pursuit. And yet, from somewhere, she was happily sure, he would find the strength when it was needed. That surging confidence in him enabled her once more to fight off terror as the captor from which she had been freed came into her mind.

"Is he following, Jack?"

"I've been wondering that same thing," Driscoll said in a tight disturbed voice. "I can't

believe that brute has sense enough to follow
a trail he can't see. And we've certainly out-
distanced him. I can't believe either that he
will go back to the village just because he re-
members you. He ought to want to stop to eat.
He must be as hungry as we are, and in a beast
hunger comes ahead of everything."

"If he really is all beast," Ann said in a low
tone.

"If?"

She was silent for a moment. Then she said
in a voice which she could not keep steady:

"Jack! It was horrible being in his hands.
You can't imagine such hands, unless they
have really touched you . . . felt you, as
though trying to puzzle you out.

"And sometimes, from the way he looked at
me . . . from the way he carried me carefully
up in the crook of his arm instead of dragging
me along, as he did at the start . . . I wondered . . . I thought . . ." Her voice went up
on a note of hysterical terror.

Driscoll put out a steadying hand.

"Forget about Kong!" he ordered. "He's no
mystery. And if you weren't so tired, you
wouldn't think so."

"Maybe I wouldn't," said Ann, and drew
close to him under the water.

They glided along, white shadow and dark
shaft, beneath the soft rays of the moon. The
current grew steadily less rapid, and the ef-

fort to make progress increasingly hard. Once, in spite of her protests, Driscoll made Ann go to a bank and rest. A very brief rest. He had insisted, but when she obeyed he was on edge until they got off again.

"See how the banks are drawing apart," he whispered after a time. For some distance they had spoken seldom and in whispers. Apprehension was growing in them both.

"We are near your lagoon," Ann hazarded.

Shortly it became plain that they were. Their drifting progress became imperceptible and Driscoll cautiously guided them both ashore.

Once there he lifted Ann's tired body in his arms. Her protests were faint. Securely cradled, she admitted her exhaustion and fell drowsily against his breast. Her eyelids slipped down as he strode away from the shore into the shadowed thickness of trees and brush. There was a deep comfort in the pressure of his arms, in the occasional grazing touch of his head upon her soft shoulder. She kept her eyes closed until he put her down.

"Just resting a minute," he whispered.

They were in a dense growth, and in the shadow of a great tree, but even there the moonlight penetrated a little and he shifted to put her body, so betrayingly white, out of the faint light.

"All right," he whispered, and picked her up again.

He rested three times more. When he made the fourth stop and her feet touched ground, Ann found they had come back to the stream. Its current was apparent again. The lagoon was behind them.

"What was that?"

Driscoll stiffened. Far to their rear, they heard a crashing in the forest.

"It might be anything, of course," he said abruptly. "But let's go."

Ann knew that he did not believe it might be anything. She knew that he believed that it was Kong. Horror stole upon her again.

Swimming, she found that this horror gave her new strength. She was less tired, too, after her rest in Driscoll's arms, and the immersion seemed to revive Driscoll. They swam steadily. When Ann lagged, he made her put a hand on his shoulder and so carried her along. That went much better than the old program of floating.

Ahead they heard a faint liquid murmur. At the sound Driscoll touched her exultantly.

"Remember!" he whispered. "I told you this water led by the chute down to the Plain of the Altar? That's the chute we are hearing."

The murmur grew more distinct.

"It's going to be tough," he whispered. "Almost as bad as the water tunnel, Ann. But we daren't delay long enough to go down by the trail along the bank."

"I'm not afraid," Ann said.

"Brave lady!"

"I'm really not. But you stay close, Jack."

"I'll be right there."

Now they saw tumbling dark water ahead.

"Easy does it," Driscoll said.

Behind them the crashing in the forest came again. It was still far behind, but they both heard it distinctly. The menace of it urged them ahead.

The tumbling stream whirled about them, swept them down the water chute.

It was over in a moment, but this time, in the brief descent they both suffered, Driscoll's right arm hung down, numb and bleeding; Ann's white thigh was streaked crimson from hip to knee, when they clambered out onto the shore.

"Is it broken?" Ann whispered at sight of the loosely swinging arm.

"Just numb; and the cut isn't anything at all. But Ann! You're hurt."

"The poor girl hasn't a bandage, either!" Ann laughed, looking down ruefully at her virtually non-existent clothing. "But what does it matter? Look, Jack! Look!"

Across the black plain, beyond the dimly visible bulk of the altar, rose a long shaft of light. It required a second look to make clear what it was . . . torch light showing through the slightly opened gate.

"They're waiting for us!" Ann cried. "Jack, oh, Jack! We're safe!"

Standing still, hands clasped, they stared in relief and thanksgiving. Then, stooping, Driscoll cradled her weight into his good left arm and marched toward the beckoning torches.

Once, as they went through the darkness, Ann thought that she heard again a faint crashing up on the precipice, but it was very faint and she heard it only once. She put it out of her mind and rested, exhausted but at peace, against Driscoll's breast.

Chapter 17

Lumpy saw them first. There had been so much talk about this big black brute called Kong that Lumpy felt a trifle jumpy. It was all wind, of course; all just so much jaw exercise. The idea of grown men holding to such a notion! But just the same it wouldn't do any harm to ramble over to the open gate and take a look out onto the consolingly empty plain . . .

Lumpy strolled with studied nonchalance over to the gate. And what he saw sent tingling currents through all his dry old bones. The plain was by no means empty. Not by a long nautical mile!

"Yo-o-oh!" Lumpy howled and tacked through the gate as fast as his surprised, ancient legs would take him. "It's Miss Ann! And the mate!"

Denham cut short his confident praise of Driscoll, forgot his philosophical summation of Beauties and Beasts, and ran. Englehorn swallowed a freshly cut half-inch of plug cut, but in spite of this he was the third man out into the Plain of the Altar. Behind swarmed a delirious, shouting train of sailors.

Just in front of the altar, close enough so that the longest rays of high-held torches picked out his drenched, sagging figure, walked Driscoll. In Driscoll's arms was Ann whose white, still form opened the sailor's mouths wider.

"Gott sei dank!" said Englehorn, finally coughing up his plug cut. And the measure of his gratitude was indicated by his use of a language he had discarded for English these twenty years.

"Jack!" cried Denham. He turned to the sailors with the air of a man who had just scored a personal triumph of the first magnitude. "By God!" he roared. "Didn't I tell you Jack would bring her back if anybody could?"

No one disputed that. Eyes popping, tongues loose at both ends, the crew trotted around Driscoll and Ann pouring out an unintelligible confusion of relief. All save Lumpy! He promptly got back his customary manner, blunt and casual.

"Lively!" he snapped. "Some of you mud-hens take Miss Ann from the mate before he falls in his tracks. Can't you see he's dead beat?"

"Give her to me!" Denham said.

Englehorn pulled out the bottle from which Denham had taken his pick-me-up earlier. It still held something. He went over to Driscoll as Denham turned toward the gate with Ann. The mate took a long swallow and shuddered.

"Do you good," Englehorn murmured.

"I got her!" Driscoll said hoarsely. "I got her, Skipper."

"Good man, Mr. Driscoll."

"Good man, my eye!" snapped Lumpy. "Great man!"

Driscoll, helped by the liquor, turned a broad smile in Lumpy's direction and plodded ahead surrounded by a back-slapping ring of sailormen.

Ann had been stretched out in the council square upon a hastily built bed of coats and whatnot. Driscoll knelt stiffly and tried to pour the remainder of the bottle's contents down her throat. She swallowed a spoonful, choked and pushed the bottle away.

"Pretty stiff stuff for her," Englehorn murmured.

"I don't need anything," Ann gasped, sitting up. "I'm all right." She caught at Driscoll and hid her face against him. "Oh, Jack! We're really back." She began to sob.

"Now! Now!" Englehorn soothed her. "Of course, you're back. And we'll have you on the ship in no time."

"Cry away, honey!" whispered Driscoll. "You've got a cry coming."

"It's the first time," he said to the others, "that I've seen even a tear from her."

They had all been so absorbed in the miraculous return of Ann and Driscoll that no one had noticed the returning natives; but the whole tribe was filtering back. At first a single woman had peered from her hut at the reunion out on the plain, and then had slipped out of sight. Other women had followed to stare in unbelief. Then one had gone swiftly to the dark outskirts of the village. And now the men, led by the chief and the witch doctor, were edging slowly into the council square. Some, with newly lighted torches, were climbing to the top of the wall.

Englehorn was first to see the pressing black mass and he whipped about with a sharp command.

"Bado!" he ordered. "Stop!"

The sailors were prompt to encircle Ann, but it was immediately plain that the natives meant no trouble. They were simply puzzled and, like their women, unbelieving. They stared at Ann and blabbed low and monotonously:

"Kong . . . Kong . . . Kong . . . Kong . . . Kong . . . Kong . . . Kong."

"That," said Denham emphatically, "is just what I want to know, too. What about Kong?"

"What about him?" Driscoll asked.

"I came here to make a moving picture," Denham replied. "But Kong is worth all the movies in the world. Now Jack and Ann are safe, I . . . want . . . that . . . beast!"

The crew, Englehorn, and Driscoll who was holding Ann in a close embrace, all stared.

"What?"

"He's crazy!"

"Don't he know when he's got enough?"

"I mean it," Denham insisted. "We've got our bombs. If we capture him alive . . ."

"No!" Driscoll burst out. Concealing the portent he had read in the distant crashing sounds which had followed him and Ann on the last stages of their flight, he faced Denham in denial. "Kong is miles away. In his lair. And that's on top of a cliff an army couldn't get at."

"Not if he chooses to stay there," Denham agreed. "But will he choose?"

"Why not?"

Denham eyed Driscoll meaningly.

"Because we've got what Kong wants. You're the man who knows that, Jack, as well as I."

"Something he'll never get again, Denham. If you're planning to . . ."

"To use Ann as bait?" Denham banished. "Not a bit. You know better than that, Jack. But you know, too, and so does everybody else, that when I start a thing I finish it.

"Well!" His gaze circled, challenging one man after another. "I've started to get my hands on Kong. And I'm going to see it through. The Beast has seen Beauty so I won't have to use bait. He'll come without any. His instinct, the instinct of the Beast, is telling him to stay safe in his mountain. But the memory of Beauty is in him. That's stronger than instinct. And he will come."

Driscoll stood up with Ann in his arms.

"I'm taking her back to the ship," he said.

High on the wall, in that instant, the murmuring monotone broke into a terrified cry, and the torches swept in broad warning arcs.

"Kong! Kong!"

From the dark plain beyond the wall came a deep, swift drumming and then Kong's thunderous defiant roar.

Ann screamed, and Driscoll held her closer.

"He's followed her!"

"Close that gate," Denham shouted. "Bar it!"

Englehorn held Lumpy and several other sailors to form a guard for Ann, but all the rest raced for the gate. Half a hundred suddenly frantic natives followed.

The two great doors began to close slowly. But already through the narrowing gap the torchlight uncovered Kong's racing bulk; and his deep rolling shout aroused a shriller wail of terror upon the wall.

The gap at the gate had become scarcely more than a wide crack when Kong's charge struck home. Before it the crack spread again and Kong's foot squeezed through. As deft as any hand, that closed upon the bottom of one massive door and thrust prodigiously. The mob upon the wall whimpered and panic swept the council square.

Driscoll disappeared with Ann behind the first hut. Denham ran up to reinforce the crew at the gate. The gate gave. Inch by stubborn inch the crack grew wider. Kong shot an arm through, groped, found a sailor, swung the man high above the heads of his comrads and crushed him to death against the barrier.

At that the natives who had been posing the massive wooden bolts, ready to shove them home when the two doors joined, wailed in defeat and ran.

Kong turned himself into a battering ram. Again and again and again he swung his shoulder against the logs of the barricade. The broad iron hinges began to rip. Under a fresh battering they tore loose with a harsh rending sound. The massive gate fell inward with a majestic deliberation.

The sailors scrambled shrewdly to safety on either side but a press of natives, fleeing straight to the rear, were crushed wholesale beneath the descending mass.

Kong filled the aperture, his body in a crouch, his eyes peering above the little men at his feet to the dark huts.

"The bombs!" Denham shouted. From one flank he gazed unbelievingly at the bulk of the invader and raced back. "The bombs!"

Kong lumbered forward to begin a slow patient search of the dark village. Over the cluster of huts darkness was now complete save for such moonlight as filtered through the trees. The last native had thrown away his torch and fled to the deceptive shelter of his home or out into the encircling brush. Kong ripped off the top of one hut after another, stooping down to peer into each. At first he only rumbled an impatient disappointment but as he met repeated failure his tone sharpened to fury.

Denham, by a wide swinging run behind concealing huts and trees, finally interposed himself across Kong's line of advance. Gripping a prized bomb in either hand, he kept his distance watchfully. A score of sailors, all armed now and a few carrying bombs in addition, supported him. Driscoll, with Ann and the small bodyguard, had already hurried through the outskirts of the village and was plunging beneath the far too bright moonlight toward the beach and the boats.

"He hasn't seen us yet," Denham told the sailors as Kong halted at another hut. "You men break back to Driscoll. I'll follow. If Kong chases I'll bomb him, but I'd rather not, yet. So many huts might stop the drift of the gas cloud."

The men ran, Denham, a wary, backward-looking last. Kong shredded another hut, uncovered a cowering family of natives. Insensate massacre followed. Denham paused as the screams reached him, then ran on helplessly.

Kong kept up his methodical quest. When he emerged at last from the village Driscoll had got Ann almost to the boats. The moonlight, however, was so bright that the two were in plain view.

Drumming upon his chest, Kong began to run at a spraddling speed which ate up the intervening distance.

Denham called out and the sailors formed a thin blocking line between Ann and her monstrous pursuer. Forward of this Denham took a stand, his hands still holding the bombs. Beside him Lumpy waited with two more.

While Kong was still far away the first bomb

landed squarely on his line of advance. As it broke a thick vapor rose and enveloped the beast-god from head to foot.

Denham raced back, turned and threw again. Kong plunged into and through a second cloud, and a third.

By now he was no more than a hundred yards from where Driscoll hurried Ann into a boat, but his great speed was gone. His deep challenging cry changed into a strangling cough, his head swung from shoulder to shoulder and his gait was no more than a staggering walk.

"What did I tell you?" Denham cried.

Recklessly the director stepped close enough to break a fourth bomb so squarely against Kong's chest that the liquid in it soaked into the thick hair and evaporated in a cloud which stayed with Kong as he struggled blindly on.

One slowly swinging hand of the beast-god grazed Denham and knocked him down. Both hands rose toward Ann, now almost within arm's reach. Unable to lift his heavy feet Kong groped, swung in a wide circle and crashed to the sand. Prone, his body still made a figure of incredible bulk in the moonlight.

"Man the boats," Englehorn ordered. "We'll get out of this.

He ran to pick Denham up.

"Are you hurt?"

"Me? Not a bit! Come on, we've got him."

"We'd best get back to the ship, Mr. Denham."

"Sure! Send some of the crew. Tell 'em to fetch anchor chains and tools."

"You don't dare . . ."

"Why not? He'll be out for hours. Snap into it."

"What are you going to do?"

"Chain him up, and build a raft to float him out to the ship and the steel chamber."

"No chain will hold . . . that."

Denham squared his shoulders, cocksure and buoyant.

"We'll give him more than chains. He's always been king of his world. He's got something to learn. Something man can teach any animal. That's fear! That will hold him, if chains alone won't."

Bursting with elation, he swung his hand up to Englehorn's shoulder and shook him impatiently.

"Don't you understand? We've got the biggest capture in the world! There's a million in it! And I'm going to share with all of you. Listen! A few months from now it'll be up in lights on Broadway. The spectacle nobody will miss. King Kong! The Eighth Wonder!"

Chapter 18

The crowd jammed four full blocks above
Times Square and spilled over into the middle
of Broadway. Traffic cops shook hopeless heads,
twiddled helpless fingers and wearily motioned
taxicabs into the side streets above and below.
Where the crowd pressed thickest, filling not
half but all the street, a sign hung high announcing to the world in fiery letters:

KING KONG
THE EIGHTH WONDER

Beneath the sign silk hats from Park Avenue jostled derbies from the Bronx, Paris gowns

rustled against $3.98 pick-me-ups, sweaters
rubbed dinner coats, slanted caps from Tenth
Avenue scraped tip-brims from Riverside
Drive. The Social Register was there, and as
representative a delegation from the under-
world as ever collected anywhere except at
Police Headquarters on a morning after a
clean-up. Intense young women from Green-
wich Village were there, and their earnest
younger sisters from Columbia Heights. There
were newsboys, peddlers, traveling salesmen,
clerks, cashgirls, stenographers, débutantes,
matrons, secretaries and Lilith-eyed maidens
with no visible means of support. The whole
town was there, waiting for the laggard attention of the ticket-taker and meanwhile staring
up at:

KING KONG
THE EIGHTH WONDER

"What is it?" asked Tenth Avenue, from under a tilted cap.

"Some kind of a gorilla, they say," replied
Park, from beneath a silk hat, tilted too.

"No! All this uproar just for an ape?" demanded Tenth Avenue, a little doubtfully.

"Hones', Kid," said a Bronx derby, "it's
bigger'n an elephant. That's what I hear straight
from a guy who knows the brother of a stage

hand right on the inside."

"Oh yeah?" said the $3.98 pick-me-up frock, "does it do tricks or what?"

"My dear!" murmured a Paris gown. "What a rabble!"

"Did you hear that?" hissed a Riverside Drive tip-brim. "Twenty bucks for an orchestra seat; and that dame calls me rabble."

Around back, at the stage entrance, a wise old doorman made way for Ann with an admiring attention he reserved for the best ones. A very different Ann from the Ann of Skull Mountain Island.

Ann had a Paris gown, too, of shimmering, virginal net. It reached all the way down to her silver-buckled toes. Only her white shoulders and arms were uncovered, these and her shining, honey-gold hair.

"Let's not go near the stage, Jack," she urged, "I don't like to look at him. Even if he is chained. It makes me feel the way I did that awful day on the island."

"You oughtn't to be here," Driscoll said moodily. "But Denham insisted. Said he needed us both for the publicity."

It was a different Driscoll, too. A Driscoll in a dinner jacket and more slender than on board the Wanderer. A smoothly shaved Driscoll, but still holding to the dark, youthful swagger.

"I'm glad to be here," Ann insisted, "if it

helps. I don't forget all I owe Mr. Denham. Besides, it is helping us, too."

"Maybe! But somehow I can't quite believe things are going to go quite so smoothly as he believes. Something is going to happen. I've got a hunch."

"A hunch! Who's got a hunch?"

Denham swung through the stage door. A very different Denham, indeed. A Denham in tail coat, silk hat and impeccable gardenia. A brisk, shrewd Denham intent upon estimating his hard-earned profits.

"Hello, Jack," said this Denham. "Hi, Ann! You're just in time. And you both look great. Holy Mackerel, Ann! I'm certainly glad we blew ourselves for that outfit of yours."

"It was terribly expensive!" Ann's eyes sparkled as she remembered how delightfully expensive it had been.

"We can afford it, sister. Ten thousand dollars in the box office. How's that for one night?"

Driscoll whistled.

"And this is just the starter. Night after night after night it's going to be just the same, only better."

Out at the stage entrance the wise old doorman was standing up against a dozen odd newcomers wearing the sort of clothes that newspapermen wear at work, which is the sort of clothes bankers, doctors, store managers and the better grade of bootleggers wear at work.

"Yes," he was agreeing placatingly, "I know you all, gentlemen. The Sun, The Herald-Tribune, The Times, The World-Telly. But how *can* I let you in? Especially when you've brought along a lot of hell-charging photographers? Mr. Denham hasn't given me any orders."

"Let 'em in, Joe," Denham called.

"The newspaper crowd," he explained to Ann and Driscoll. "Here for interviews with you two. And maybe I wasn't smart to break the interviews right with the opening of the show and get twice the splash."

"Have you ever been interviewed, honey?" Driscoll asked, hot and red.

"Just for a job," Ann murmured. "But this can't be worse."

"Miss Darrow, gentlemen," Denham said waving an introductory hand. "And Mr. Driscoll, the Wanderer's heroic mate."

"Boy, oh boy!" hissed a photographer. "What a break the mate got when he rescued her!"

"I hear you had a peck of trouble, Mr. Driscoll," the Times man said.

"Don't make any mistake about that," Ann interposed. "He was all alone when he did it. All the sailors with him had been killed."

"I didn't do much," Driscoll insisted, running a finger around a suddenly tight collar. "Denham's the one who got Kong. The rest of us were going backward fast, but Denham had the nerve to stand and chuck bombs."

"Don't drag me into this," Denham protested shrewdly. "Miss Darrow's the real story. If it hadn't been for her we'd never have got near Kong. He came back to the village to get her."

"Beauty!" exclaimed an inspired tabloid reporter. "Beauty and the Beast. Boy, what a headline! I'll cut me a slice of bonus for that one."

"Beauty and the Beast!" Denham repeated admiringly, and winked with satisfaction at Ann and Driscoll. "Exactly. That's your story."

"What *we* came up for," said a photographer impatiently, "is pictures."

"In just a little while," Denham promised. "I'm going to let you take some pictures right on the stage. After the curtain goes up and the audience can watch. The first pictures, gentlemen, ever taken of Kong for publication anywhere in the civilized world. And you may snap Miss Darrow and Driscoll standing right alongside."

"Hot-cha!" said a camera man through his nose. "This is going to be good."

"So far, yeah!" said another. "But how'll it be if this guy Lyons, of The Sun, pulls his usual stunt of crowding his camera in front of the rest of us?"

"Who, me?" cried the man called Lyons. "Why, I'm practically figuring on frenching this job. You don't have to worry about me. My boss, Bartnett, wouldn't do much with a picture like this."

"Not much more than four columns," agreed the tabloid photographer.

"Tell me this," the Sun's skeptical reporter interposed. "Are you sure that you've got your twenty-foot ape tied up good and tight?" He spoke with a Missouri drawl and teetered on his toes with the light stance of a good squash player. "I ask," he added, "because I'm wearing my best suit and I don't want to have it torn."

Denham's laughter rang with solid reassurance.

"Take a look for yourself." He motioned them to the wings of the darkened stage.

Kong was there, a king no longer. He crouched in a great steel cage under a weight of tangled chains. Chains led from his hunkering body to ring bolts in the thick steel floor. Chains held his great paws immovable and bound his broad black feet. Only his head was free. That swung mutely upon his audience. As Denham quickly explained, he had not used his throat for any speaking purpose for days, and his hands were too tightly bound to drum now upon his chest.

"Just the same," said the Sun's skeptic, "if you don't mind I'll let the more eager news gatherers go first."

"Ann!" Denham beckoned. "And you, too, Jack. I want you both out on the stage when the curtain goes up."

"Oh, no!" Ann shrank back, her face as white as her gown.

"Come along, sister," Denham urged genially. "It's all right. We've knocked a lot more of the fight out of Kong since you saw him last. He's harmless."

Reluctantly, Ann joined Driscoll at the edge of the stage. Kong swung his vast head toward her. The photographers began arranging their cameras and electric flashlights.

"If I can catch that honey-girl right up alongside the ape," said a tabloid photographer, "the paper'll spread it all over P One."

"I hope the ape is really tied tight," said the Times reporter.

"Oh, sure! This Denham's taking no chances. Not with a gold mine like he's got."

Denham patted Ann's arm reassuringly.

"It won't be long," he said. "I'm going out to make a little speech. Then the curtain'll go up. You two will pose. And after that, just as soon as you've told the newspapermen a little more, you can go back to your hotel."

Ann was thankful her hotel was nine blocks away. When Driscoll engaged a room in one just across the street from the theater she had marvelled at his recklessness.

Denham edged out past the curtain with a

cheerful flip of one hand. From there his voice came back to the group on the shadowed stage. The reporters and camera men waited with the scant patience of those to whom speeches are no treat. Ann drew close to Driscoll and sighed gratefully when he put an encouraging arm about her waist.

Kong's deep-set eyes watched the arm, and his chains rattled faintly.

"Ladies and gentlemen," came Denham's voice. "I am here tonight to tell you a strange story. So strange a story that no one will believe it. But, ladies and gentlemen, seeing is believing. And we—I and my associates—have brought for your eyes the living proof of our adventure; an adventure in which twelve of our party met terrible deaths."

The Sun skeptic nudged the reporter from the Times.

"That twelve isn't any Tammany count, either," he said. "It's the real thing. McLain, who covers ship news for us, slipped onto Denham's boat disguised as a columnist and got the same count from an old sailor grand-dad, an A. B. named Lumpy."

"My paper said only nine were killed," the Times man disagreed.

"The other three weren't fit to print," the Sun skeptic explained cheerfully.

"But before I tell you any more, ladies and gentlemen," Denham's voice went on outside

the curtain, "I am going to let you look for
yourselves. I am going to show you the greatest sight your eyes ever beheld. One who was
king and the god of the world he knew, but
who now comes to civilization as a captive, as
an exhibit to gratify mankind's insatiable curi-
osity. Ladies and gentlemen! Look upon Kong,
the Eighth Wonder of the World."

The curtain rose and the audience surged to
its feet as one. Murmurs, gasps, frightened
stifled cries ran through the theater. Denham
smiled the showman's smile of triumph.

On the stage Kong's head swayed and his
chains began a faint but continued jingling,
as though he were trembling.

"And now," said Denham reaching into the
wings for Ann, "let me introduce Miss Ann
Darrow, the pluckiest girl I've ever known.

"Here," he went on as the audience settled
back to applaud, "is Beauty. There is the Beast.
Miss Darrow, ladies and gentlemen, has lived
through an experience no other woman ever
dreamed of, about which I shall tell you later.
She was rescued from the very grasp of Kong
by the Wanderer's brave mate, Mr. John Driscoll."

Driscoll, red and reluctant, stood beside
Ann, and the audience, conscious that they
were gazing upon romance, murmured approval of the slim, bright-haired girl and her
boyish, swaggering partner.

"Lastly," Denham went on, "before I tell you the full story of our adventure, the newspaper photographers are coming on the stage and you, the first audience to look upon Kong, will have the privilege of seeing taken the first pictures of Kong since his capture."

Kong's chains continued that faint jingling as the camera men tramped nonchalantly out before the footlights. The man called Lyons slid nimbly into a position which the tabloid reporters eyed resentfully.

Denham drew Ann close to the cage. She pleaded silently, but tried to hide her fear when he shook his head warningly. The photographers, in a whispering chorus, urged her to smile and she did her best. The flashes exploded dully inside electric light globes and the stage was filled with a blinding glare.

Kong curled his mobile lips back from long white teeth and then, unexpectedly, he roared. For the first time in days he found his voice. As his rolling thunder re-echoed deafeningly from the ceiling and the audience started up, Driscoll's mouth tightened apprehensively. Ann stifled a cry and drew back a step so that the mate was between her and the cage. Denham, however, laughed loudly in reassurance.

"Don't be alarmed, ladies and gentlemen," he cried. "Kong's chains are of chrome steel. He'll stay where he is."

The thunder of Kong's voice fell to a distant muttering, but his chains now were jingling more loudly.

"Stand close again, Miss Darrow," the camera men urged.

The blinding glare once more filled the stage. Ann shrank away, covering her face with her hands. Driscoll looked impatiently toward Denham.

"It'll be all right now, Ann," he said. "I guess we're through."

"Wait!" Denham ordered. "One more, together."

The white glare flashed across the stage a third time. Kong opened his mouth and roared from deep in his chest. As Driscoll swung an arm protectingly around Ann the captive beast-god struggled furiously. His rage was a wild and cataclysmic emotion which surged from his inmost being.

"Holy Mackerel!" Denham whispered. "He thinks you're attacking her, Jack. Hold it! Hold it!" And he motioned excitedly to the photographers.

Kong stood up. The great body which had been held by chains to a crouch was suddenly and terribly erect. Kong's head struck the top of the cage and tore it loose. His hands, dangling broken bits of chain, began to drum upon his broad chest. One enormous foot, rattling both chain and ringbolt which an instant before had held it to the floor, pried at the scarcely resisting bars which separated him from Ann.

Panic threw the audience into a shouting, screaming tangle. By scores and hundreds they clawed one another seeking passage to the exits.

Driscoll swung Ann into his arms and broke through the startled newspapermen toward the stage door. Behind him the steel bars snapped and Kong's roar shook the theater's walls.

"My hotel!" Driscoll cried into Ann's ear. "Just across the street."

"Let me down," Ann gasped. "We'll go faster if I run."

They raced along the narrow alley which led from the stage entrance and got to the sidewalk. Across the street, at the revolving door of the hotel, Driscoll glanced back. Kong was just bursting out of the stage entrance.

"Elevator!" Driscoll cried, and raced Ann inside.

As they drew breath behind the closing elevator door Kong crashed into the hotel lobby. A hotel detective emptied a revolver into the monstrous intruder and looked incredulously at his weapon when Kong swung around in undiminished strength and crashed back to the street.

Chapter 19

Behind the locked door of Driscoll's room Ann sank upon the bed.

"I can't stand it, Jack! I can't! It's like a horrible dream—like—being back there—on the island."

"We're safe here. I won't leave you, honey. They'll get him. It's going to be all right."

Driscoll knelt down and when she cried with thick, racking sobs he pretended to laugh at her.

"You mustn't begin to cry when the trouble's all over."

Ann wiped her eyes with a slow, woebegone hand.

Driscoll, laughing still, leaned toward the nearest wall and motioned Ann to follow.

"Here! Here's something to make you smile. Listen to what's going through the telephone in the next room."

. Drawing her close to the locked, intervening door he made her attend to a shrill, night club soprano voice on the other side.

"Yeah, Jimmy! It's Mabel . . . You bet I'm glad you're back . . . Talk louder, Jimmy. There's fire engines going by . . . Sure, I saved the evening . . . Ten o'clock'll be swell . . ."

"We oughtn't to be eavesdropping like this," Ann demurred.

"Shucks!" said Driscoll. "If it cheers you up, why not?"

". . . And say, Jimmy, wait till you see me in my new outfit . . . It's a wow, kid . . . All right . . . Sure, I'll be there . . . Say, when did I ever break a date with you, Jimmy boy? . . . Absolutely! With bells . . . Ah-h-h-h!"

Driscoll's subdued mirth vanished as the monologue ended in a high, strangled scream.

"Oh, my God! Jimmy! Jimmy! Ji——"

Driscoll leaped from his knees for the door. He had got it only half unlocked when Kong's black arm thrust through the window. At Ann's cry Driscoll turned and seized a chair. Kong knocked him senseless against a wall with a wide sweeping movement, jerked the bed to the window and lifted Ann through. Cradling her in one arm with that curious care which had marked the previous capture, the beast-god leaped from the side of the hotel wall to the top of the adjoining building. Driscoll staggered to the window just in time to see the huge dark shape swing out of sight across the roof-tops.

"Denham!" he shouted senselessly. "Denham! Where are you? Can't you stop——"

He ran back to the door and blundered down the corridor to an elevator.

In the streets below New York was mobilizing for a fantastic, grim pursuit. From a score of waiting posts police radio cars raced toward the hotel, their sirens screaming for clear traffic lanes. A hundred police nightsticks rapped the pavements and aroused a hundred more. Far south on Centre Street a dozen motorcycle cops, with Tommy-guns, careened out of Headquarters, and in their wake rolled the multiple-cylindered automobiles of the Department's highest.

". . . How did that brute ever break loose? Those chains should have held an army tank . . ." ". . . Get some fire trucks! This is going to be a ladder job. . . ." ". . . Clear the streets! Get everybody off! Everybody . . ."

Driscoll thrust the elevator operator aside and got out of doors just as Denham, surrounded by policemen, came breathlessly around a corner of the hotel.

"He went up the side of the hotel, officer!

Don't shake your head, you damned fool! He
did. That beast can climb smooth marble."

"Denham!" Driscoll cried. "He got her."

Denham stopped short and raising clenched
fists, shook them above a torrent of profanity.
One of the policemen hiked up his coat tail
and hauled out a revolver. The police radio
cars streamed in, six at a clip through the
cleared lanes.

"Look!"

The packed throng in front of the hotel
spoke with a prolonged single voice.

Two blocks down the avenue Kong appeared momentarily on a rooftop, in the glare
of an electric sign. Ann was a small white
patch in the crook of his left arm. The policemen fired uselessly as the beast-god swarmed
up the side of a higher building and disappeared.

"Everybody pile on this fire truck," shouted
a sergeant; and then to the driver he commanded, "On your way, waterboy!"

Driscoll was aboard, and Denham, too, as
the truck whirled in pursuit.

"Keep going!" the sergeant ordered. "He was
going east, toward Sixth Avenue. Go a block
past where we saw him and stop."

Kong was nowhere in sight when the riders
leaped down to look; but a taxi-driver ran
across the almost empty street under the dark

elevated structure and waved still farther east.

"It jumped!" he screamed, still refusing to believe his own eyes. "It jumped. From that building there, to the L tracks, and from the tracks to the building on the other side."

"Scatter!" shouted the sergeant. "Circle the whole block!"

Far to the east, crossing Madison, were yellow headlights in front of screaming sirens. The quick-witted fire-truck driver sounded his own signal, and the yellow headlights raced forward and stopped. A stuttering string of motorcycles followed and close behind the police commissioner and a carful of his inspectors.

"Will machine gun bullets kill that brute of yours, Denham?"

"Enough will, I guess."

"Is he cornered?"

"We lost him right here, sir," the sergeant said.

From the distant eastern side of the block came the sound of shots.

"I circled some men around there, Mr. Commissioner," the sergeant cried.

"After him!"

The cars swung into Sixth Avenue, tore down the block, whirled east against the one-way traffic signs and slid to a stop on screeching brakes. The motorcycles swung in front, on either flank, and in the rear, like torpedo boat destroyers around a battleship. Last came the rumbling truck. At the corner of Fifth Avenue a shaking policeman pointed south. But in that direction Kong was not to be seen.

"If only we knew of a place he might be heading for!" the Commissioner cried.

"I can make a guess," Driscoll said ruggedly. "It'll be some place high up. Kong is used to mountains. He lived in one. The higher he is, the safer he believes he is from his enemies. If there's any building in this district that towers over everything else, that's the building we'll find him on. On the very top of it."

"So that," said the Commissioner slowly, "is why they ran the Empire State Building up a thousand feet and more."

"Rot!" said the blunt chief inspector.

"Driscoll's right," Denham interposed. "That's our best bet."

"I guess it's our only one," the Commissioner amended. "Let's go."

By now a dozen reporters had gathered, and a crowd which packed the street. The Commissioner shouldered through these to his car, Denham and Driscoll following his beckoning hand.

"There! There! Down there!"

The great host gave tongue.

Kong appeared for the third time since he had made his capture. Again he was far down the street; again he crouched a brief instant on the roof of a building and again disappeared.

"Let her out," said the Commissioner, and his car swept away to where the square tower of the Empire State lifted its crown up through an encircling veil of white light.

They reached the building's corner just in time to witness a scene which no one of them believed, even though he sat watching. From a roof on the upper side of the street, Kong leaped. His black, monstrous body curved in a long arc, clear across the roadway to the lowest section of the sky-scraping structure opposite. And then he pulled himself, from windowledge to windowledge up the first setback and disappeared.

By the time Driscoll, Denham and the Commissioner had leaped out, the beast-god was swarming up the next setback.

"Don't shoot," said the Commmissioner. "He's still got the girl."

There was no mistaking that. Ann rested in the arm Kong did not use for climbing.

"Send some of those Tommy-guns up the elevators," the Commissioner ordered. "He'll never climb to the top. We'll maybe catch him on the roof of one setback or another."

Driscoll struck down the Commissioner's pointing arm.

"You'll never catch King Kong on any roof," he cried furiously. "He's going to the top of the mountain, I tell you."

"Easy, Jack," Denham said.

"It's true. Look! There he goes up again."

Kong was so high now that his figure seemed smaller than that of a man, and still he climbed. A black silhouette against the chalky walls he drew himself from ledge to ledge until he rose into the bright floodlights which swept around the crest of the building and still he crawled.

"That means the end of the girl," the police sergeant said. "If we shoot him up there, she's gone."

"Wait a minute," Driscoll cried. "There's one thing we haven't tried."

The Commissioner looked at him.

"The army planes," Driscoll explained, "from Roosevelt Field. They might find a way to finish Kong off and leave Ann untouched."

"It's a chance," said the Commissioner. "Call the Field, Mr. O'Brien. Burn up the wires."

"I'm going up into the building," Driscoll announced, loosening his collar. "I'll take a try at Kong's mountain myself."

"I'll go along, Jack," Denham offered.

The Commissioner motioned to half a dozen

police officers armed with sub-machine guns and they followed.

"Let me take one of those things," Driscoll demanded when they were inside the cool corridor of the building.

The policeman caught a nod from his sergeant and handed the piece over.

"I can use it," Driscoll assured him. "Denham tell him how good I am."

"The boy's good," Denham said. "Plenty good," he added hoarsely.

There was a fair delay after they got to the last elevator level. The keys to the door which led to the observation platform were missing and the custodian had to be found.

"Listen!" Driscoll whispered.

From far off they heard the drone of a plane, of a squadron of planes.

"The good old Army!" Denham said, trying to laugh.

The planes came into sight, tipped with green and red lights, six of them, high in the air. They were far higher than the top of the skyscraper. They were so high that their red and green lights almost merged. One after another, they hurtled down beneath the stars.

Kong roared overhead and the drum note of his fists rose to a wild tattoo.

"We can see from here," Driscoll said and led the way through a window to the farthest corner of the small roof which belonged to this topmost setback. Above them, on the ledge of the observation platform, Kong roared his challenge as the zooming ships swept down.

Ann, in her shimmering white dress, lay between his solidly planted feet.

The second plane had cut in close, obviously meaning to brush Kong with a wing tip. As the plane curved, its wing missed. It was Kong who struck the blow. His great paw swung out and struck. He staggered; but the plane, torn out of its path in the air, crashed down, bounded from the wall, and then spun out and down to the distant street. Halfway in its flight it burst into flames, and this illumined infinitesimal figures which swarmed around as the wreck struck.

"They're coming back," Denham said. "The whole five are circling back."

"And this time," Driscoll prophesied, "they'll shoot. There's room. When Kong rises to challenge and beat his breast Ann is so far below they can pump at his chest and not risk hitting her."

"About all we can do is pray, I guess," said the sergeant.

"You can pray if you like," Driscoll told him. "But I'm going out. I can wait behind the door that goes out onto the platform. When Kong gets his, I want to be close."

Denham said nothing, but he followed; and so, after a short uncertainty, did the policeman.

By the time Driscoll got to the door the planes were zooming back, and Kong was giving them his whole, infuriated attention. His great feet gripping the parapet, he flung his roaring defiance to the night wind.

High up among the stars, the red and green lights of the leading plane twinkled, then suddenly rushed downward.

Kong pounded his chest, stretched to his highest stature.

Driscoll unlocked the door, opened it a crack and waited.

The plane came down in a long swift slide. For a split second it seemed to poise, like a giant humming bird, in front of its beast adversary; then it curved upward and was away. But in the instant of pause its machine gun had poured lead into Kong's breast.

Driscoll, watching, could have sworn he saw the bullets jerk Kong's coarse hair as they plunged into his heart. Kong staggered, and one lifted foot, brushing Ann, rolled her off the parapet back onto the roof space.

Kong turned slowly, as though he meant to pick her up. His lifted foot settled back. He stopped, staring down at Ann with a puzzled, hurt look. He began to cough.

From high in the night, the other planes swooped down. Kong's challenge broke upon a harsh, rending cough, but he straightened to his greatest height and his drumming tattoo was as loud as ever.

One after another the planes slid down, poised each for its successive murderous instant, and then curved away. The rattle of the successive machine guns grew louder over Kong's tattooing. He swayed, and in spite of his gripping feet, began to topple.

He fought to the end. With his last strength he leaped for the rearmost plane as it curved away. He missed, but his mighty spring carried him clear of the setbacks below, and out above the street. For a breath then, high above the civilization which had destroyed him, he hung in the same regal loneliness that had been his upon Skull Mountain Island. Then he plunged down in wreckage at the feet of his conquerors.

Driscoll swept Ann into his arms.

"Ann! Ann! You're all right."

Ann lay against his breast crying in soft thankfulness.

Denham and the sergeant leaned over the parapet.

"Well!" said the policeman. "That was a sight. I never thought the aviators'd get him."

"The aviators didn't get him," Denham replied slowly.

"What?"

"It was Beauty. As always. Beauty killed the Beast."

The sergeant's puzzled frown grew deeper.

D(